Gaia Girls

Enter the Earth

Gaia Girls

Enter the Earth

By
LEE WELLES
ILLUSTRATED BY ANN HAMEISTER

Daisyworld Press

ISBN 1-933609-00-1

Library
of
Congress
Cataloging
-in-
Publication
Data on file.

Printed in the United States of America.
100% Post-consumer Recycled Paper.

-For Baba Sonia-

We miss your smile, laugh & generous spirit.
If I could send a copy to heaven, I would.
I hope you will read over my shoulder instead.

Acknowledgements

Writing a thank you page is a daunting task. So I guess I will start at the beginning. I would like to thank my father and all the Welles that came before me on our family farm. (Eight generations!) What a gift to grow up in such a place! I want to thank my mother for giving me a childhood awash in imagination and creativity. You made that farm come alive! My big sister, Ann, is the one who brought this book to life with her illustrations. I have always been a little jealous of your artistic talent, but now am simply grateful for it! You also asked great questions that prompted great revisions.

Now I get to my husband, Jay. Thank you is a tiny phrase to offer for all that you have given me. As a teacher, you knew that children would love this story and without your pestering, I may never have glued my butt to the chair to write it! The look on your face when we finished reading that first draft aloud to each other is forever etched in my mind. Your endless hours of editing were heroic. Your willingness to flounder along with me through the publishing process is one of the many things that earns you the title of my best friend.

To the scores of friends and family who read and proofread this book, thank you too. And yes, I am working on the next one! Father Steven Loposky, my spiritual advisor and fellow enthusiast of the classic themes in the human experience, thank you for your great suggestions--even though they created more revisions on my part!

I would be remiss if I didn't share the deep feeling of gratitude I feel to be in such an interesting and ever-changing world. Gaia is a constant companion who I see in the blue sky above, the soil below, the water, the trees and every creature who crosses my path.

Thank you.

Contents

1
Home is Where the Heart Is

Sometimes the strangest of times begin in the most normal way. Elizabeth's eyes told her it was still night, but her ears knew better. Mourning doves could be heard outside the window cooing and staking an early claim to the day. The grackles and starlings began to tune up, the finches added their high notes, and the music of a new summer day had begun.

Elizabeth flared her nostrils and smelled a deep, rich, earthy smell. She knew that there was a cold wet fog lying like a soggy blanket across the farm. She looked out the east-facing window on her right to see if there was a hint of sunrise. The sun was up, but as yet, unseen. It would still be a few hours before the sun would climb over the ridge and summon the strength to lift the fog up into the sky where it would become the day's clouds.

Elizabeth hunkered deeper into the warm sheets and blankets, enjoying the cocoon of body heat against the remains of the chill night air. She heard rustling and low talking coming from her parents' bedroom. No one in the Angier household used an alarm clock in the summertime. They all went to bed at night knowing that there were a hundred jobs that were most comfortably done in the early hours before the sun and the mosquitoes joined forces. Such was summer on a farm.

It's not quite officially summer yet, Elizabeth

thought as she swung her legs out of bed. Her feet landed, as they did each day, on a large pile of fur. The fur grunted and big brown eyes turned to look up at her. "Good morning Maizey! Lazy Maizey! Get up, you big ox!" Elizabeth rubbed her feet a few times across the side of the large Bernese mountain dog, both to warm her feet and prod the dog into action. Downstairs came the sound of the coffee grinder and the twin thumps of her dad shoving his feet into his large Timberland work boots. Maizey followed Elizabeth to the closet.

"Well Maizey, what do you think I should wear today? Only two more days of school left! Two days and then we can hang out together all day. What do you think about that?" Maizey's tail thumped up and down exactly twice. Elizabeth took that as the dog version of "Sounds good to me!"

As always, as Elizabeth came down the stairs, the smell of coffee was drifting up to meet her. Her father liked to joke that the only reason he could get his tired body out to the barn at such an ungodly hour was the thought of hot coffee waiting for him back in the

3

house. Elizabeth went to the bread box, as she did each day, to start slicing bread and making toast. It was only this school year that her mother had let her start using the big bread knife. It had been a surprise for her on the very first day of school.

"Seeing as you're a big fourth grader now," her mother had said, "I think you are big enough to use a knife in the kitchen. We will start with bread, because it will teach you to be careful and by the time we're bringing in cucumbers next July, you will be slicing and dicing like a New York City chef!" Elizabeth had felt excited to be able to do one more thing to help.

It made her feel good when her father had said, "Yep! It's a good thing to know how to use a knife." She had felt big.

She was startled to notice, for the first time, that her hand on the knife was now much bigger than it was the first time she had gripped the black handle. *A lot of things change in fourth grade*, she thought. She was mulling over everything that had changed during the school year when her mother said, "Elizabeth! Are you expecting company for breakfast?"

Elizabeth looked down at the cutting board to discover she had sliced almost the whole loaf! "Sorry Mom, I was thinking about stuff."

"End of the school year, I'm free to swim all day and eat blueberries until my tongue turns blue kind of stuff?"

Elizabeth smiled. "Yeah, something like that." She didn't think her mother wanted to hear about the girls in her class that had started to get weird: the girls that no longer played kickball at recess, but huddled, giggling and whispering, around Tiger Beat or Teen People magazine. Thank God her best friend, Rachel, had not 'gone over to the dark side,' as they liked to call it.

Most of the time they didn't even know what it was that the 'dark side' girls were talking about. Rachel didn't even have a television at her house and Elizabeth's parents only allowed her to watch an hour a week. Elizabeth had tried to persuade them to give her more time. "I would watch a lot of nature shows if I could watch more," she had argued.

Her father had grinned at her and told her to come

outside with him. She had followed him up into the woods where he squatted down next to a fallen tree and said in a big booming announcer's voice, "Welcome to TREE T.V.!"

He had showed Elizabeth that there was a whole world going on beneath the log. There were beetles and worms and salamanders, all scurrying to and fro on some important tree business. He told her if she came back each week for a new episode that she would learn more than the television could ever teach her.

Rachel and Elizabeth now had several places they viewed Tree T.V. They had, together, watched a robin raise a nest of chicks, watched a fallen apple tree turn into a hollow log and then checked the dirt around the log each week to see what animals were using it to hide out. She was looking forward to having more time in the summer to observe such interesting things.

Elizabeth's mother spoke. "Don't let me forget to ask Will to stop by after school. Your father needs a little help today and there's five dollars in it for him."

"I can help!" Elizabeth said, feeling indignant that her father needed a rent-a-son.

"Sweetie, you're always helpful, and I know your father appreciates it, but some jobs take more muscle than intention. Will is simply older and stronger than you."

Will Jeffries lived on a small dairy farm that was on the other side of the hill. He was a senior. Well, really, he was already a grownup and done with high school, depending on how you looked at things when there were only two days of school left. Elizabeth liked him. He never treated her or her friends like little kids. Sometimes, if they passed in the hall, he would give her a wink and a smile. She was glad their school was what is called, a 'central school.'

Avon Central School housed all the children, K-12, that lived, mostly, along the fertile river bottomland of the Avon River. There were many streams that fed into the Avon. The river and the streams were all surrounded by big green hills that steered the water and pushed the air. There were some kids who lived on small farms up in the hills; others lived in identical box shaped houses, lined up side by side outside of town. Subdivisions, her mother called them. And there were a few kids living in what looked like castles. These castle-houses were sometimes bigger than her barn! They were perched on various ridgelines, positioned for maximum view of the farms below.

She had heard her parents laughing about the lords and the serfs when they talked about those castle-houses, but she wasn't sure what that meant. She did know that the kids who lived in those houses never rode the school bus, but were dropped off and picked up in large, shiny sport utility vehicles. "Utility vehicle!" she had heard her father snort on more than one occasion. "You don't put leather seats in anything that has a utilitarian purpose!" Elizabeth had wanted to ask what 'utilitarian' meant, but looked it up on Yahooligans instead. When she saw the definition, she understood. Her dad had the same pickup as long as she could remember and boy did he utilize it! It seemed the SUVs mostly ran the castle dwellers up and down the hills.

Elizabeth had heard some of the girls that had gone over to the dark side giggling about being in love with whichever boy from whichever boy band. Elizabeth had a love of her own. She loved her farm. Although she didn't really think that thought, in those specific words, she felt it in the way her heart got bigger every time they passed their sign and turned up the long driveway. The farm was called Three Oaks Farm, after the three imposing old oaks that made a perfect line through the middle of the farm. It was a long gone relative, a Revolutionary War soldier who named the farm. He also named the grand oak trees.

The first oak stood where their long driveway, 'the lane' they called it, met the road. They called that oak tree 'The Sentry.' Elizabeth remembered in second grade learning to use a dictionary. She had looked up sentry, and found out it was someone who guarded. That is what The Sentry seemed to do, guard their farm. It was so big that it took three people to wrap their arms around its great trunk. From the lowest branch hung a large wooden sign that said, "Three Oaks Farm Est. 1782." This sign made it easy for people to find their farm. Each year Elizabeth and her father took it down and repainted it so that the green and yellow lettering stayed bright.

The second oak tree was between the house and the big barn. From that tree's branches hung a tire swing for Elizabeth and a two-seated bench swing for her parents. That tree was called 'The Chaplain.' Her father said this was because it knew how to listen and not judge. Elizabeth wasn't sure what that meant, but The Chaplain was a constant presence in her life. This was the tree that creaked and groaned when the wind was high, created deep shade in the summer when the sun was high, and was a favorite perch for the mourning doves' sunrise sonatas when they wanted to be high enough to dominate the birdsong landscape. Although it was not as tall as The Sentry, its branches spread almost the width of the backyard. The yard was kept shaded and cool and many family occasions were celebrated under the arms of The Chaplain.

The third oak was all the way at the top of the hill. When you looked up, you could see it towering over the other trees along the ridge that was the property line between Three Oaks and the Jeffries' farm. The third oak was called 'The Scout.' Like an army scout, it seemed to have taken a high position and now tirelessly watched the movements in the valley below. The Scout had a series of boards nailed into it like a ladder. It allowed one to climb up to the lowest branches where a small platform was constructed. Her father told her that her great uncle had built the steps and platform. This was a favorite reading place for Elizabeth and she always sent a thought of thanks to the long-dead uncle every time she climbed the ladder.

Perched in The Scout's platform, she could see their whole farm spread below. She especially enjoyed the view during the long summer twilights. As the sun lowered in the sky, she could look down the long slope of their hillside and see her mother as a small speck bent over in the vegetable garden or her father on the tractor in one of the fields. The sound of their small herd of sheep would rise out of the pasture like a sad song about another summer day gone. She could see The Chaplain bestowing its blessing of shade behind the house and The Sentry standing guard and marking the end of the lane.

There was a fourth large oak tree on the other side of the ridge. It was in line with her three oaks and resided smack dab in the center of Jeffries' corn field. Her father joked and called it 'The Turncoat.' That was because in the Revolutionary War, if someone changed sides, they called that person a turncoat, for changing and wearing the coat of the other army. It was said in fun because the Jeffries were good friends with the Angiers. Will Jeffries said that maybe those trees were so old they remember the Iroquois Indians. Maybe the Indians purposefully left those oaks in a line as guide-posts. Elizabeth liked that idea and liked to think that once, long ago before the European farmers came to clear the woods, there had been a great line of oaks, nodding and waving to each other and passing infor-mation up and down a living line all through Upstate New York.

Elizabeth's father came through the back door into the mudroom. "Look what I found straggling down the hillside." He laughed as he sat to take off his muddy boots.

Will Jeffries came in the door, cheeks flushed pink from the walk over the hill and across their pastures. "Norton gave me a bit of a run this morning!" Will said.

Norton was a cranky old ram who didn't take kindly to folks getting too close to his ewes. "Ya ready Lizzy?" Will said, as he scooped up a piece of buttered toast.

Will was the only person Elizabeth allowed to call her Lizzy. She didn't like any of the shorter versions of Elizabeth. But when Will called her Lizzy, it sounded like something an older brother would call his little sister. And, since Elizabeth had no brothers or sisters, save Maizey, she cheerfully accepted the nickname. It might bug her that her father needed a rent-a-son, but at least with Will it was like borrowing a brother too.

2
Dell Danner

"Two more days! Two more days!" Elizabeth began chanting as she grabbed a sweatshirt and her backpack. Will and Elizabeth headed through the living room and out the front door. Maizey sat inside the screened porch and whined a little as they cut across the circular drive and headed down the lane.

As they walked, Elizabeth continued to sing softly to herself. "Two more days! Two more days!" In the fog-laden hayfield, two young white-tailed deer and the mother doe picked up their heads and looked at Elizabeth and Will. Their bodies were alert and tense and Elizabeth couldn't resist. She called across the field to them: "Hey! Just two more days!" She laughed at the flash of their tails as they turned and bounded out of sight.

"Happy to be done with school?" Will asked.

"I'm happy to only have two more days of waiting for the bus with Dell Danner!" Elizabeth replied.

Dell Danner lived on the farm adjacent to Three Oaks. The Danner farm was a pig farm and when the wind was from the west, the pungent odor of thousands of pounds of pig, pig feed and pig excrement was carried with it. Thankfully, the wind most often came from the south. On days the wind did come from the west, Elizabeth's father could be heard saying, "Good thing Danner is too lazy to raise more than a few dozen hogs!"

Dell was the oldest of the Danner children and he didn't smell much better. There were a lot of Danner children. Dell was in the fifth grade, his little sister, Debbie, was in the fourth grade, but not in the same class as Elizabeth, Dave was in the third grade, and Don was in the second grade. Duke was in kindergarten, but had missed so much school due to recurring ear infections, that the Danners decided to home school him the rest of the year and have him do kindergarten over again.

The first year Elizabeth had ridden the bus to school, Dell had been thrilled to have someone new to pick on. Debbie had quietly looked on while Dell had teased and tormented Elizabeth at the bus stop every day. He stepped on her feet to scuff her shoes. He pulled her braids. He sat on her backpack to squish her lunch. He made up such memorable rhymes as "Lizzy Angier wears no underwear." Debbie was undoubtedly delighted that she was no longer the main focus of Dell's creative energy.

It took Elizabeth three months to get up the nerve to complain to her mother. She somehow thought that her mother would simply keep her home from school to keep her away from Dell, and Elizabeth loved school. What her mother did was contact Mrs. Danner and, after that failed to produce any meaningful change, called Mrs. Jeffries and arranged to have Will come over the hill each morning and wait for the bus with Elizabeth and Dell. Will was so much bigger and older than Dell that Dell didn't do anything except tease his sister for the next year. Each subsequent year he had one more sibling to victimize while they waited for the school bus.

The Danner children were adept at fighting back and it was easier for Elizabeth and Will to stay out of the crossfire. The only time Will stepped in was when the squabbling actually came to blows. Once, after Dell unwisely punched Will in the gut, Will actually popped Dell right in the nose and made it bleed! Elizabeth had told the bus driver that Dell fell and hit his nose on Will's elbow. The other Danner children happily agreed with her. Dell had muttered threats to Will for the next two days, but for the most part, kept his distance and kept his torments verbal.

Today was no different. When they reached the end of the drive, Dell was tossing Debbie's backpack up and down in the air while she whined and jumped and tried to get it back. Elizabeth and Will took their normal spots on the far side of The Sentry's trunk. They had just shaken off their own backpacks and leaned against the tree when they heard a wet splat and a cry of, "Hey, that's my lunch, you bonehead!"

When they looked around the tree, Dell was fishing out another food item; it looked to be a peanut butter and jelly sandwich. He cocked his arm back and, SPLAT, it was creamed up against the Three Oaks Farm sign right next to what might have been a peach before it had became a tool of Dell's teasing.

"Hey!" Elizabeth yelled as she rushed around the tree. "That's our sign; cut it out!" Dell grinned, ducked past, and grabbed her backpack.

"Maybe you have something to contribute?" he said as he ripped back the zipper and pulled out the brown paper bag.

"Come on, Dell," Will said as he stepped forward.

Dell backed up closer to the sign as he rummaged

through Elizabeth's lunch bag. With a mocking sneer he said, "Oooh! Homemade cookies! Aren't they special!" He turned to the sign and smeared the chocolate chip cookies across the face. Elizabeth was stunned. She opened and closed her mouth a few times trying to muster words to express her outrage. It was one thing to tease her, but he had defaced her farm!

Dell turned back toward her with a smug look on his face. Elizabeth could hear Will walking up behind her muttering under his breath. Normally she was happy to let Will fight the Dell battles, but this was about Three Oaks. This was about disrespecting her farm. She didn't need a rent-a-brother.

She set her mouth in a tight line. She narrowed her eyes and she took a deep breath that seemed to go down into her feet and into the ground. She intended to open her mouth and call him a few choice names, but as she began her exhale, something remarkable happened.

The branch on which the Three Oaks sign hung pulled back and swung forward. The sign, on its two-foot chains was a half step behind. THWACK! The bottom of the sign clipped Dell neatly in the back of his head and he went sprawling face down into the dirt.

There was a moment of silence. The insult that Elizabeth had been conjuring up came out, instead, as a laugh. Will joined in. The other Danner children hid their smiles behind their hands, as they had long ago learned not to raise the ire of Dell any more than necessary.

"Get up, you big bully!" Will said as he picked up Elizabeth's lunch, deposited it back into her pack and handed it to her. "The bus is here."

Elizabeth couldn't resist giving his foot a kick as she walked past and she looked over her shoulder at Dell long enough to stick out her tongue. His normally narrowed eyes were wide and he was rubbing the back of his head. His face, shirtfront and knees were smeared with dust. He either didn't see Elizabeth stick out her tongue or ignored it to raise his gaze up to the oak's branches.

As the bus pulled away, Elizabeth twisted in her seat and looked back. Through the spun gold of the early morning fog, she could see The Sentry; it merrily waved its branches and she swore she heard a low, long chuckle.

3
Beginnings & Endings

School was rowdy that day. It was the last 'real' day of school. Mrs. Foster had declared the day a clean-the-classroom and movie day. The day after that was field day, where they spent the day outdoors engaged in various races and contests. It was always a fun way to end the school year. Everyone hoped that they got to ride the bus home holding one of the ribbons that were given out for first, second and third place.

When Elizabeth headed down the aisle, she saw that Rachel was in the seat next to hers. Rachel Winters had been her best friend since kindergarten. They both were ferocious tree climbers, master rock skippers and shared a distaste for most things girly. They had started out the school year sitting side by side, but had been separated for talking and passing notes. They still passed notes, but had to go through two other students to do so.

Right now Rachel was literally bouncing up and down. "Guess what! Guess what!" Rachel said, grinning so broadly Elizabeth could see her back teeth. "What?"

"I'll give you a hint. M.I.C.K.E.Y...." She had an expectant look on her face.

"You finally got a horse and his name is Mickey?" Elizabeth guessed. Rachel lived on a farm that was on the other side of the Avon River. Rachel's family grew corn and not much else. Rachel was always lobbying her parents for a horse, but met with a steady, no livestock policy.

"No, guess again!" Elizabeth could tell that Rachel was about to explode with news. She started to open her mouth with another guess when Rachel burst out, "My parents are taking us to Disney World in Florida! They told me last year that if we ever went, I could take a friend if they could pay their way! Do you think you can? Will your parents let you? You and me in Florida!"

She started clapping her hands as she relayed the last bit of information. Elizabeth stood there letting the news sink in. Airplane? Florida? She had only been out of New York State twice, once to visit her Aunt Marie in Toronto, Canada and once to Connecticut to a funeral for someone she had never met. She was only five at the time and didn't remember much about Connecticut except the fancy furniture and the smell of lilies in the funeral home.

"You're serious?" Elizabeth began to smile at the thought.

Rachel jumped up and grabbed Elizabeth's elbows.

She jumped up and down and began singing "M.I.C......K.E.Y." Elizabeth joined in: "M. O. U. S. E!"

Becky Newman pushed passed them and said, "Disney World is for babies."

Elizabeth and Rachel looked at each other, looked at the retreating back of Becky Newman and then looked back at each other. Elizabeth shrugged, Rachel shrugged, and they both burst out laughing. Being best friends, they each knew what the other was thinking: *"Who cares what Becky Newman thinks!"*

They spent the first half of the morning cleaning out their desks, filling a large trash bin with the leftovers of their learning. Mrs. Foster put a movie on to fill the rest of the morning, but most of the kids talked over the movie and got out of their seats.

Elizabeth forgot about school altogether. She was looking out the window at the blue sky and wondering what the sky looked like from an airplane. She looked at the grass and wondered if the grass in Florida was different. She looked at the trees and wondered if palm trees were the only kind of trees that grew in Florida. She knew that whenever she saw pictures of Florida, they usually had palm trees in them. *But oranges come from Florida.* Elizabeth thought. *So there must be orange trees, lemon trees too.*

Elizabeth knew a lot about trees since that was one of her jobs on their farm, tending the tree nursery. And she was good at it. Her father said he never knew anyone with such a green thumb. "My trees have all been happy and hardy ever since she was big enough to carry a watering can," she had heard him boast to customers. "If I could be certain that all my progeny would be so gifted, I'd have ten kids!" Elizabeth felt her cheeks glow when she heard that. She figured a green thumb was something that a boy might not have, so it was a good thing to be a daughter.

But right now Elizabeth wasn't thinking about the young cherry and maple trees that would eventually adorn the yard of some bloated castle-house in a swanky neighborhood downstate. She was thinking about palm trees and oranges and airplanes. She was so deep in thought that Rachel had to poke her in the shoulder to get her attention. "Aren't you hungry?"

Elizabeth was hungry. She had a brief flashback to

her chocolate chip cookies being the victim of Dell Danner. She had planned on telling Rachel about the cookies and the sign when she got to school, but the news of a possible trip to Florida had knocked the incident out of her mind as surely as the Three Oaks sign had knocked Dell Danner on his face.

They spent lunch sitting knee to knee deciding how to best approach Elizabeth's parents. Elizabeth knew it would be a challenge since, like most children who grow up on a farm, she was part of the labor force that made the farm run smoothly and profitably. Elizabeth's farm, although it was small, was more profitable than most in the area. Instead of producing large quantities of a single item, Three Oaks grew a variety of produce and boasted that it grew them organically.

The Angiers didn't use chemical fertilizers or pesticides on their farm. Her father said their job was to use what Mother Nature supplied to keep the soil healthy. Her mother kept careful track of the seeds they used. Heritage seeds, she called them. The Three Oaks website explained that heritage seeds were good old fashioned vegetables that had not had the flavor bred out of them in favor of a long shelf life or speed of growth.

Chefs and chefs' assistants from New York City were always the first to their stall at the farmer's market on Saturday. A few even paid extra to have mid-week deliveries. The restaurants they worked at boasted about the organic food and, her mother informed her, people could taste the difference. Elizabeth had once heard Chef Ramone, of the famous Ramone's Café, say, "It may look low rent, but it tastes high class."

Elizabeth knew exactly what he meant. Their vegetables were often oddly shaped or had funny bumps or colors, but the flavor exploded in your mouth and was a beautiful thing. She had heard it said that her mother had a great deal to do with the success of Three Oaks. She had been an advertising executive in New York City before meeting her father and knew how to 'teach the customers what they need;' at least that is how she often put it. Her mother also used a computer to keep track of what Three Oaks had and she e-mailed her best customers ahead of time. Unlike many at the Market who had to sit all day to sell their produce, the Angiers often had everything pre-sold. This was how confident their customers were of the high quality of the produce that their healthy soil grew.

Three Oaks also sold the wool from the sheep. The Angiers and the Jeffries had a sheep shearing party every June. They spent two days wrestling the sheep into Sing Song Creek for a washing and later, when the wool on the sheep had dried, got them into a small holding pen and held them still to have their fleece cut off. The site of the sheeps' skinny, pale bodies always made the Jeffries and the Angiers laugh. Elizabeth thought it was all great fun. The sheep bleated in protest, but in the end, the storeroom was full of rolled up bundles of fleece that were waiting to be carded, spun, dyed and made into skeins of soft wool that would be sold both on the Internet and in specialty knitting stores all over the country.

Elizabeth ran through her list of chores and tried to figure out how to negotiate a one-week release from her duties. Would Will be able to water the trees for her? Maybe she could bribe Dell Danner to come over a couple times to run the push tiller between the vegetable garden's rows and remove the weeds to the compost pile. It was early in the summer, so there wouldn't be much in the way of picking or packaging. She might be able to get Debbie Danner to pick and arrange wildflowers. This was Elizabeth's own part of the Farmer's Market. She would go out and pick a variety of blooms such as Queen Anne's Lace, Black Eyed Susan, Chicory and Goldenrod and arrange them in small bundles to be sold for $4 each. She often made $50 or $60 a week.

Elizabeth doubted that Debbie would know how to find the best blooms, ones that would open in their perfection in three days, and she would probably be terrible at arranging them, but desperate times called for desperate measures. She really wanted to go to Florida.

All the way home on the bus Elizabeth ran over the conversation she would have with her parents at dinner. Elizabeth, Will and the Danners spilled off the bus; Dell gave the Three Oaks sign a sideways glance and a wide berth, but still managed to give Debbie's hair a yank and trip little Don with his foot before he took off at a jog down the road.

Debbie Danner rubbed her head and smiled a little at Elizabeth and Will. She pulled Don up by his shoulder, swatted the dust of his clothes and muttered, "Come on." Don stuck his tongue out at her and then ran ahead, smacking the back of Dave's head as he ran past.

As Dave, Debbie, and Don ran off, the normally quiet road erupted into screeches of, "I'm telling!" "Knock it off!" and "Stay out of it!"

The Danners made their way down the road with insults and dust swirling around them. Elizabeth watched as they faded into the heat haze.

"Wow!" said Will. "Imagine what dinner is like at their house!" Elizabeth smiled up at him. That was Will's way, to break a tense moment with a comment that would make you smile. "What are you grinning about?" Will asked. "You've got something up your sleeve, Lizard Breath, I can tell!" Elizabeth wanted to tell him about the possible trip to Florida. But, unlike Will, Elizabeth was the kind of person who kept things to herself until she absolutely needed to speak up.

"Nothing up my sleeve, Buffalo Breath. I'm just

happy school's almost out," she offered.

As it turned out, she needn't have told Will or asked for his help because her parents flatly refused. "Why not!" Elizabeth had wailed. The explanations had ranged from, "Because we need you here," to, "We don't have the extra money for a plane ticket, hotel, and expenses."

As Elizabeth angrily did the dishes, she overheard her parents on the back porch. "I'm surprised that John and Joyce are taking the time and money on such a thing as Disney World!" her mother said, a worrisome tone in her voice.

"I know John could hire help, but I don't see how they can keep up, taking that kind of vacation time at this time of year," her father said.

Her mother replied, "Maybe I'll give Joyce a call after Little Lizbeth goes to bed."

Elizabeth was surprised to hear her mother use what she considered her baby nickname. They had called her "Little Lizbeth" until Elizabeth, all grown up and starting first grade, had insisted they call her Elizabeth. She hadn't heard them use it in over three years. It never occurred to her that they would continue to use it in private. Elizabeth was also surprised that this discovery seemed to cool the hot anger in her chest.

She finished the dishes, whistled for Maizey, who slept under the kitchen table, and set off through the backyard. She paused to give The Chaplain's great trunk a few affectionate slaps. She tilted her head up and admired the lacy pattern the leaves made against the blue of the twilit sky. The dark green against the deepening blue cooled out any lingering hot and hurt feelings she carried. She sighed and gave The Chaplain one more pat. Elizabeth passed out from under the umbrella of the oak tree's branches and veered left at the barn. She continued down the slope and past the greenhouse. This late in June, all the little seedlings, which Elizabeth had helped care for throughout the cold spring weather, had been set out and were now hearty pepper and tomato plants.

Beyond the greenhouse was the tree nursery: row after row of small trees in pots. Larger trees had their roots safely encased in a large ball of dirt and wrapped with burlap. It was imperative that these roots stay wet, dark and cool. They would most likely be delivered somewhere in the tri-state area in the next two weeks. Elizabeth knew that when she saw Frank driving the large truck down the hill, it would be time to start getting the next batch of maturing trees wrapped and ready. It always annoyed her that after all her attention and care of each tree, it was Will's muscle that helped load them on the truck. If she had been big enough to load the trees, she would tell them where they were going and wish them farewell and goodbye.

But for now, her job was to make sure that the trees were well-watered. She turned on a spigot and started to unwind a large roll of flat hose. Maizey walked along with her, nosing about and panting loudly. Elizabeth stopped at each tree and placed her palm on the root ball. Her father had taught her to feel for a certain moistness and temperature, but what Elizabeth felt for was thirst.

She could sense when the tree was seeking water. It always made her feel good to open the hose and soak the root ball. She could feel the tree's relief and had gotten into the habit of talking to each tree while she watered it. She figured if she enjoyed conversation at the dinner table, why wouldn't the trees?

"My, you are looking tall and strong today," she said to a paper birch. "I love the way the breeze makes your leaves sing," she commented to the aspen. It was only when she approached the last tree and found it not in need of water that she remembered she was supposed to be unhappy.

Elizabeth turned off the hose and sat with a thump on the root ball. Maizey flopped down at her feet and set her great, wide, black nose in between her paws with a sigh. Elizabeth also sighed. *It's not fair!* she thought. She felt the heat of her anger beginning to rise up. *All I ever do is water these dumb trees! I never get to go anywhere! I HATE trees!*

A breeze came up and stirred the leaves of the red maple she was perched on. "*Shhhhhhhhhhh. That is not true. You love us and we need you.*"

Elizabeth jumped up and looked around. The voice was strange and deep and had seemed to come from directly behind her or maybe in front of her, or it might have been above her. She didn't know where it had come from, but it scared her. Maizey, sensing her fear, jumped up as well and issued a little growl and then looked up questioningly at Elizabeth as if to say, *What are we growling at?*

"Come on, Maizey," Elizabeth said. She rolled the hose as fast as she could and then hurried up the rise and through the backyard. She was almost running as she passed the trunk of The Chaplain.

She didn't see her mother sitting in the swing and issued a little yelp when her mother called to her. "Slow down there, kiddo! I need to talk to you!"

She walked back to the swing with her head down and her wet sneakers making a little squeaky squish as she walked. She turned and sat next to her mother without ever looking at her. "I think you are really disappointed about Florida. Maybe you're even mad at your father and me?" Elizabeth didn't reply.

"I called Rachel's mom." Elizabeth felt her heart jump and she looked up at her mom with wide, expectant eyes. "Honey," her mom continued, "I have some news for you. Maybe I should wait and let Rachel tell you. But, quite frankly, I would rather see you sad than mad. Rachel's family is moving to Orlando. Her parents planned the trip to Disney World as a way to soften the news. She apologizes for Rachel getting your hopes up. They're telling her tonight."

Elizabeth kept staring at her mother and could see her mom's eyes searching her face for a response. Elizabeth's mind began to grasp what her mother had told her. She shrugged her mother's arm off her shoulder and jumped off the swing.

"THEY'RE MOVING?" she shouted.

"Honey, I know this is upset...." her mother began.

"RACHEL IS MOVING?" Elizabeth shouted again. Her own voice surprised her a little. It popped out with an intensity that seemed to make the leaves above her twist and bend.

"Elizabeth, I know you're upset, but please don't shout. Let's talk." But Elizabeth didn't hear the rest. She turned on her squishy-sneakered heel and took off running.

4
It Sounded Like

She could hear her mother calling her name and saying something about it getting dark. She didn't care. She ran down past the barn. She ran over the bridge that spanned Sing Song Creek and didn't even stop as she always did to look at the water. She climbed over the fence to the sheep pasture and kept running. She was vaguely aware of Maizey running at her heels, but she didn't care. Dimly she sensed the herd of sheep running away, bleating in alarm at her wild movement, but she didn't care.

She pumped her arms harder as the sheep pasture began to rise up the hill towards the great expanse of woods. By the time she reached the edge of the woods, she was breathing hard and thinking, *I don't care! I don't care!* over and over. She climbed the fence and began to hike up the steeper trail through the trees. As her panting slowed, she knew she was saying that to herself because she cared so much, she thought her heart would break.

Soon she reached The Scout, the great oak that was on top of the hill. Dusk had deepened; the wood had become graduated blues and blacks. Day animals scurried to get home safely and night animals came out to meet them. Elizabeth saw none of this because tears had filled her eyes and spilled over to her freckled cheeks.

She climbed the tree using the boards nailed in as

steps and flung herself down on the platform. She cried for about five minutes before sitting up. She had never liked crying. It was such a girly thing to do. She wiped her eyes with the back of her hand, stood, and gazed out across the valley below.

The sky to the east was already dark with night; to the west, a band of brilliant red and purple graced the skyline of rolling hills and was reflected in the Avon River. She could hear the sound of Maizey pacing anxiously around the base of the tree. She felt thin and empty, so she leaned into the solidness of the The Scout's trunk and gulped a few times. Her feet were very wet and getting cold. She had wet feet and her best friend was moving. Her best friend was moving and she had wet feet. She felt very sorry for herself. She closed her eyes and leaned her cheek against the rough bark of the oak.

She could feel the slightest swaying motion of the The Scout's trunk. The evening breeze caused a rhythmic creak in its branches. It was almost as if the ancient tree was rocking her and shushing. She wasn't sure how long she stood, leaning and listening, but she soon became aware of a different sound. Folded into the creaking of the branches was the rhythmic squeak of the dual swing that hung in her back yard. She could hear low voices, faded, as if they were down a long corridor. She pressed her ear tighter to the oak and strained to identify the voices.

"I'm sure she'll be back soon. It's dark, and if I remember correctly, our Little Lizbeth doesn't relish traipsing about in the dark." It was her father's voice! Then it was her mother's.

"She was really upset. I'm really upset! I thought there would be more town council meetings before they would go buying up the whole darn valley! How many farms have they acquired?" Her mother's voice sounded scared. Elizabeth wondered who "they" were.

"Well, it doesn't matter! I am not moving!" her mother said. It was startling how quickly her voice went from sounding scared to sounding steely and resolute. Elizabeth could hear a tough city sound in her voice.

Her father soothed, "Julia, we're not moving. I hear they're staying focused on the upper end of the valley, closer to the Interstate."

"Exactly! All their filth and chemicals will come downstream and pollute our little slice of heaven! I won't stand for it! I won't!"

Elizabeth started to shake; partly from the chill of wet sneakers and drying perspiration, and partly from hearing a conversation she was sure she was not meant to hear. Her knees felt like jelly and began to knock. *Hey! How am I hearing this?* her inner voice finally questioned. And with that thought, her eyes popped open.

She was still standing on the platform high in The Scout on top of the hill. Her parents were 600 feet below her in the valley. She couldn't possibly have heard them. *I'm hearing things because I'm upset about Rachel! Rachel!* Elizabeth felt her heart tug as she remembered the news of her best friend's impending move, and in her belly she felt the lead weight of guilt for having only thought of herself. Rachel must be finding out that she really was moving! Her best friend was leaving!

Elizabeth turned and hurried down the ladder.

Maizey turned happy circles, ready to get home. Elizabeth walked and jogged down the wooded path. To the left of the path there was a shallow ravine. The banks were steep in places, covered with plants such as trout lilies, trillium, and ferns. The small runoff stream that had carved the ravine typically dried up by the end of July. It rolled and bounced down the hillside and curved toward the path where the path met the fence of the sheep pasture. It then followed the fence line before taking a sharp turn just behind the barn. The little stream reached its conclusion, where it added its water to Sing Song Creek: an appropriate name since it gurgled and sang all year round, save for the coldest winter months. Sing Song, in turn, made a winding path, wreathed in willow and cottonwood trees, down to the river.

Elizabeth was ducking under the fence at the high end of the sheep pasture when a movement near the edge of the ravine caught her eye. In the deepening twilight she could not make out its form. She quickly called for Maizey and held her collar fast. Dusk was an active time for many animals. Critters of all sorts were either waking up and heading out into the night, or heading home to safe shelter for sleep. It could be a porcupine, a raccoon or a skunk: none of which she wanted her dog to tangle with!

Maizey's ears and eyes were riveted to the form, but oddly she didn't have the tension in her body that she normally had when about to give chase. Nor did she growl. She had the happy forward-looking posture she did when friends of the family came to the farmhouse door.

The movement revealed itself as an animal that was long and sleek and scampering along the bank. Elizabeth could barely make out its silhouette. In an uncharacteristic move for a dog that loved to give critters chase, Maizey sat on her haunches. Elizabeth squatted down beside her. She couldn't decide if she wanted this creature to see them or not. She forgot about her wet feet. She forgot about her best friend. Her attention, like Maizey's, was fully fixed on the ravine's edge.

The creature now stood on its hind legs. It lifted its long form up and a pointed snout sniffed back and forth through the air. It dropped back to all fours and took two hops toward them. Elizabeth tightened her grip on Maizey, knowing full well that if the large dog decided to bolt, she really couldn't hold her back. Maizey, amazingly, lay down and put her head between her paws and let out a soft whine.

The animal was now galumphing straight toward them. Elizabeth felt her eyes stretch wide when she realized it was an otter! She had never seen an otter before! Did they ever have otters on the farm? She couldn't remember her father talking about otters. Wow! Just as Elizabeth was starting to relax and smile at the thought of telling her father she spotted an otter, the sleek brown creature did something completely unexpected. The otter paused, rose up on its hind legs and began to wave its front right paw. Elizabeth saw the creature's dark sparkling eyes in the remaining light. Again, it waved its front paw.

Without thinking, Elizabeth slowly raised her right hand and gave a little wave in return. She had to let go of Maizey's collar to do so, but the dog was now happily thumping her large tail in the pasture grass and making small little whines like a puppy. The otter waved again. Elizabeth waved again. She couldn't believe it was happening and knew if she spoke out loud, the otter's instincts would cause it to turn and run back to the stream.

"Are you waving at me?" Elizabeth said in a small voice and waited for the expected flash of moonlight reflecting off the otter's gleaming coat as it turned to run. But the otter didn't turn to run. Instead, it did a remarkable imitation of Elizabeth's own mother!

It placed both paws on its hips (but of course it didn't really have hips), tilted its head down, fixed its glittering gaze on Elizabeth, and said in a high voice that sounded like the happy chirping of the small stream behind it, "Yes, I am waving at you. We have a lot of work to do. But at this particular moment, your parents are talking about coming out to find you. So, I suggest you get on home, and we will talk tomorrow."

Elizabeth's lower jaw dropped open. Her eyes were widened and her mouth went dry. She swallowed, licked her lips, and said in a whisper, "We will WHAT?"

The otter dropped back to all fours. The voice was

high pitched, but warm, like the bells of a wind chime. "I said we will talk tomorrow. Do you or do you not come up to check on the sheep?"

"I..I...I do." Elizabeth stammered.

The otter said, in a voice that sounded like the music of raindrops, "Of course you do. I've seen you. I will be here and we will talk more then." It turned back toward the stream, paused, and turned its pointy face back over its shoulder (but of course it didn't really have a shoulder). "You may hear things and you may see things before this time tomorrow. Things like trees swinging signs into the back of a rude boy's head." Elizabeth was so stunned she fell back onto her bottom. She was so stunned that she hardly noticed the evening dew soaking through her shorts, making them as wet as her sneakers.

"Be brave," the otter continued in a voice that sounded like a soft breeze. "I will explain everything." It took a few hopping steps toward the stream and then turned back again. "And try not to get upset at anybody! If you do, try to get your feet off the ground."

"My feet? I don't understand!" Elizabeth said.

"Sometimes I don't understand myself!" The otter seemed to be chuckling as it proceeded with its strange rocking gait back toward the stream. "Trust me, my dear," it said, its voice sounding like the shimmer of ice crystals. "Trust me." The otter's rump disappeared over the edge of the ravine and Elizabeth heard a small splash as the otter hit the water.

She jumped up to her feet. Maizey jumped to her paws. "Wait!" She called. "Who are you?"

In her mind, a voice that sounded like the singing of all the stars in the heavens whispered, "I am Gaia."

5
Echoes

Elizabeth stood rooted. The crystalline singsong voice seemed to echo over and over in her ears. *I am Gaia. Gaia. Gaia.* When Maizey's tail began to wag against her shins, she blinked, gave her head a shake, and finally tore her eyes away from the ravine. She looked down and Maizey too had her eyes fixed on the ravine's edge, her tail telling of her happy feelings for this amazing creature. *Gaia. I am Gaia.* Elizabeth turned and stumbled her first few steps down the hillside pasture. Her mind felt blank of its own thoughts and still rang with the music that had drifted up out of the ravine. *I am Gaia.*

Elizabeth climbed over the fence. As she crossed the creek, it seemed to echo the voice. *I am Gaia.* The barn was to her left, and through the lattice of The Chaplain's leaves she could see the lights of her house. Maizey bounded ahead, but Elizabeth took her time walking up the slope of the long, green yard. Each footstep seemed to ring the chime in her head, *Gaia Gaia, I am Gaia.* The bang of the screen door startled her and she froze in her tracks, standing beside the trunk of the great oak tree.

Her mother appeared and paused on the top step of the screen porch. Her eyes briefly searched the yard and when they fell on Elizabeth, she came off the steps and was across the yard in a heartbeat. She knelt down so that her face was level with Elizabeth's.

"Oh honey, I am so sorry about Rachel. You must..." She began in that soothing tone that mother's have, but stopped when she fully took in Elizabeth's face. "Elizabeth! What happened?" Her voice had the edge of mother's panic. She began to look Elizabeth up and down and her hands, searching for information, moved from Elizabeth's shoulders to her head to her arms and finally landed on her cheeks.

When Elizabeth saw the lines in her mother's face deepen with concern, she opened her mouth to reassure her and then closed it again. What would she say? *Don't worry, mom, I was just up in the sheep pasture talking to an otter.*

Instead, all the tension of the strange, odd day came rising up through her torso and burst out of her eyeballs in a flood of tears. Had she known then the way the strangeness would drive deeper into her life, she would have saved the tears.

Her mother smiled with understanding, stood, wrapped her arms around Elizabeth's shoulders, and guided her back toward the house. Elizabeth could vaguely hear all kinds of soft, soothing mother words about friendship spanning space and time. She knew that her mother thought her tears were for the loss of the best friend she ever had. How could she stop to explain the encounter in the sheep pasture? How could she find words to describe how the encounter seemed to have opened up a deep well of feeling?

This was the deep well that she drew from when she addressed the trees she watered. This was the deep well that was filled back up every time she took in the soft, moist smell of the willows along Sing Song Creek. Now that well was boiling up out of her in torrents of tears. She was a big, raw mass of feeling and didn't know if the feeling was sad, mad, scared, excited, or something her fourth grade vocabulary had yet to label. She just knew that the voice echoing in her head was now moving down through her entire body and had set her bones vibrating. She knew that just when she needed a best friend most, she was going to lose her.

6
Denial

Music. Beautiful music and someone humming low. Music and birdsong. Music and birdsong and humming and that low chuckle. Where have I heard that chuckle before?

Elizabeth's eyes remained closed, and she allowed herself to be rocked by the deep, resonant voice before beginning to wonder whose voice she was hearing. The wondering in her mind seemed to push the voice back into the night. She was safely in the warm cocoon of her cotton sheets. She could hear the soft cooing of the mourning doves in the arms of The Chaplain outside her window. *This is just another day, a regular day, a normal day.*

Wait! This was the last full day of school and a day of fun and games! Elizabeth took a deep breath in, sat up straight, a smile pulling on her face. She was ready to leap from her bed full of excitement when the memories of last night's events struck her like a cold dousing of water.

Her smile faded. She fell back to her pillow and felt a deep pain settle in between her eyes and take up the cadence of her heartbeat. She moaned as the pain in her forehead took on a deeper and more insistent tattoo. She curled up on her side and ignored the large, wet, snuffling dog nose that was trying to pry its way under her sheets.

No. She thought. *Rachel isn't moving. I did NOT talk to an otter. I did NOT hear my parents talking last night. I dreamed everything. Today is the last real day of class and TOMORROW is Field Day.* Elizabeth pinched her eyebrows tighter together to both stem the drumbeat of headache that was gaining momentum and to convince herself that the self-dialogue was true.

Elizabeth stayed curled up in a ball with her eyes pinched tightly shut until she heard her mother knock softly twice and the familiar creak of her bedroom door hinges as her mother came in.

"Elizabeth? Sweetie? It's time to get up!" Her mother's voice had a false brightness to it that seemed to increase the pounding in her head. She didn't move.

"Elizabeth?" She could feel her mother's hand on her hip. "Are you feeling okay?"

Elizabeth rolled onto her back but made sure the sheet stayed over her face. "I have a terrible headache." This was true. Her head felt as if her father's axe were repeatedly pounding her between the eyes. "I can't open my eyes or my skull will split open and my brains

54

will spill out on the floor."

There was a long pause. She felt the dip in her mattress as her mother sat on the edge of her bed. The silence was almost louder than the pounding in her head. Would her mother yank back the sheets and tell her to get up, shower, and get off to school? That is what she normally did if she thought Elizabeth was dodging school. Would her mother think she was faking? Elizabeth screwed her eyes up even tighter and held her breath, waiting for her mother to respond.

"I'm not surprised," her mother said in a soft and gentle tone. "Get some more sleep. It won't hurt you to miss Field Day. When you're ready, get up and we can talk." Elizabeth felt the bed spring up as her mother rose. She could hear her mother's bare feet padding across the wooden floor and Maizey's claws clicking along behind her. She heard the soft snick of the door latch connecting and only then did she let her breath out with a whoosh. The pounding in her head redoubled.

She rolled onto her back and covered her face with her pillow. She mentally followed the familiar routines of her household. She heard the coffee grinder and minutes later smelled the brewing coffee. She heard the thump of her father jamming his feet into his work boots. She heard the bang of the back screen door as he headed out for his morning chores. She smelled the eggs frying in the pan and barely made out the sound of the bread knife against the cutting board as her mother did what Elizabeth would be doing if she were up.

A wind picked up and stirred the great spreading branches of the oak tree in the backyard. A silvery whisper danced in the jingle of the leaves: *And why aren't you up, dear one?* Elizabeth sat bolt upright in bed, eyes wide and ears straining. She thought she heard the barest hint of low chuckling, but that may have simply been the sound of the oak boughs creaking. She put her hands over her face. She was sure she was going crazy. Otters didn't talk. Trees didn't laugh. And Rachel couldn't possibly be moving all the way to Florida.

Elizabeth heard the bang of the screen door and Will's voice drifting up from the kitchen below. She heard her mother's voice too. Her mother, no doubt, was saying that Elizabeth was too sick to go to school and she would hear Will's feet go past the stairwell, through the living room, and out the front door. *I bet he won't forget his toast!* Elizabeth thought.

But as she was thinking this mean thought, she heard footsteps on the stairs that didn't fit the normal sounds of her household. She heard a little cough and realized that Will was coming up the stairs! She dropped the pillow from her face and stared at the door. What was her mother thinking? She shouldn't let some boy up to her room!

"Lizzy?" Will waited for a reply. Elizabeth, being the kind of girl who didn't talk unless it was necessary, said nothing. He could assume she was asleep and that was OK with her. "Lizzy, your mom told me about Rachel. I'm sorry. I hope you feel better." Elizabeth said nothing. "Lizzy? Elizabeth?" She heard his feet shuffle as he turned, and the clump of his sneakers as he descended the stairs. She didn't move or make a sound until she heard the front door close; then she exhaled loudly and realized her headache was gone.

Her headache was gone and her best friend in the whole world would be gone too. Rachel, her best friend since kindergarten, was going to be moving to a new place and going to a new school and making new friends. Elizabeth didn't know exactly when this was going to happen, but she suddenly realized that she didn't want to waste any moment she might have left with Rachel!

She got out of bed, dressed quickly, washed her face, brushed her teeth, and practically ran down the stairs. "Mom! I'm feeling better!" Elizabeth called, as she ran into the kitchen. Her mother paused with her big yellow coffee mug halfway to her mouth.

"No more headache?" her mother said. Her eyebrows raised as her coffee mug lowered.

"No more headache!" Elizabeth answered with what she hoped was a reassuring smile. "I promised Rachel we would be partners in the three-legged race. I've gotta go to school!"

Her mother set the mug down and smiled at her. "Run or you'll miss the bus!"

Elizabeth leaned out and snatched a piece of toast

off the table. She ran two steps toward the kitchen doorway, turned, ran back, and hugged her mother. She pelted through the living room and out the front door. She could hear Maizey's excited barks fading behind her as she ran down the lane.

Unfortunately, she also heard the rumbling of the school bus pulling away from their stop. "Wait!" She yelled and doubled her leg speed. But the lane was long and by the time she had reached the Three Oaks Farm sign, the bus's taillights were two dim spots in the fog.

Elizabeth leaned against The Sentry with her breath heaving from the sprint. Her eyes stung with sweat and her mind filled with one desperate thought: *Wait! I HAVE to get to school!* Elizabeth heard a huge crunching, tearing sound and the ground seemed to twist beneath her feet. Before she could open her mouth to scream, everything went dark.

7
I am Gaia

Elizabeth felt like she was falling. Her nose filled with a moist, woody smell, and she heard the same low chuckling she had heard in bed that morning. Her body felt like it was being twisted and bent and pushed and pulled. She was on the verge of panic when the high silvery voice filled her mind. *Calm, dear heart! You are safe within me. Calm. Brave, I said. Be Brave.*

Elizabeth felt the voice, a voice that sounded like a cold spring stream tumbling down a hill. She felt the voice fill in the space that had been about to fill with panic. She took a deep breath in and when she exhaled she felt her feet on solid ground. She opened her eyes to take in an immense, dim space.

She turned around in a slow, unbelieving circle. She seemed to be in some sort of cave. The ceiling was latticed with tree roots and the floor was packed earth. There was a small stream running though it. There was a small opening near the ceiling at her right. It let in enough light to see by and a breath of sweet, fresh air. She only had a brief moment to take this all in before she realized that before her was an otter, THE otter. Again, it was standing on its hind legs and again, it had its wee paws perched on its hips.

When the otter saw that Elizabeth saw it, it dropped to all fours and shook its head with what appeared to be exasperation. The otter began to circle

Elizabeth and in a high voice that sounded like the harps of heaven said, "What did I tell you about getting upset and getting your feet off the ground?"

Elizabeth turned to follow the otter's path, and her mouth worked as she tried to think of a response. "I...I...I..."

The otter stopped and tilted its head to regard her with one dark, sparkling eye. "Listen sister, we have serious, serious work to do! I understand that you don't understand. At this point you will have to trust me. You have a gift. I have heard you for a long time and I decided it was high time for you to hear me. However, you need to listen closely and follow my instructions to the letter! Do you even know how you got here?"

Elizabeth turned her head to again take in the vast underground cavern. "I think that headache split my head open, I'm delusional in my bed, and my brains are on the floor. This isn't real. Is it?"

The otter rolled around its axis several times, laughing in a way that sounded like silver coins being jingled in a pocket. "Oh, my dear! You are certainly not dreaming. You were not dreaming when you listened to the young trees to know their thirst. You were not dreaming all the times you sat below the willows and heard the sighs of the earth. You were not dreaming when you stood in the oak and heard your parents talking. On the contrary, dear heart, you were fully awake! You, my love, you are one who loves me fully. Now, I am asking for your help."

Elizabeth shook her head, as if to clear her mind. She rubbed her eyes and blinked at the otter. The otter looked right back at her and blinked its dark, sparkling eyes. They stared at each other for a minute more before the otter turned and scampered up onto a rocky outcrop. It was at eye level with Elizabeth.

The otter sighed and it sounded like the wind through a stand of aspens. "I have introduced myself, but perhaps I should try to explain myself. I am Gaia. You see an otter because I had to assume a form that you would be willing to look at and not run from, if you heard it speak. I am Gaia. I am the whole of the earth. Do you understand?"

"I..I..I.." Elizabeth searched for words.

"I..I..I..," the otter mocked in a voice that sounded like ice shards breaking off the eaves of the roof. "Stop thinking about I! This is about WE! Do you understand that everything you know is just one living thing?" The otter rose up on its hind legs again, but now that it was up on the rocky ledge, its face was above Elizabeth's and she had to look up at it. She felt like she was in the principal's office. Her mind was swimming; her legs began to shake. The pounding pain in her head returned in a sudden, violent rush and her vision narrowed. The otter's dark, glittering eyes and twitching whiskers retreated to the end of a long dark tunnel and then everything went black.

Elizabeth heard music coming from far away. She was in the dark but felt compelled to move herself toward the most beautiful sounds she had ever heard. It sounded like harps and choirs and bells and magic. The sound grew louder and louder until it was all around her. It was then that she woke with a start and sat straight up. It only took a moment for her to realize that she was still in the cave and that the otter was still perched on the ledge regarding her with those dark, sparkling eyes.

"Welcome back, dear," the otter said. In the otter's voice Elizabeth seemed to hear elements of the music that had drawn her.

"Were you singing?" Elizabeth asked. The otter seemed to smile, if indeed, otters can smile.

"Did you like it?

Elizabeth stood up slowly. "It was the most beautiful thing I have ever heard."

The otter chuckled and it sounded like wind chimes in the breeze.

"The reason you could hear that song at all is because your ears are open. Every time you have smiled at the sound of a cardinal's call, every time you have been lulled to sleep by the rain, every time you have wrapped your arms around the oak tree and paid attention to the music of its leaves in the wind, you have been listening to that song. It is my song and I am Gaia."

"I don't understand!" Elizabeth said. Her throat was tight when she asked, "What is Gaia? How can you be anything except an otter? What do you want from me anyway? I should be at school." She sat back down on the packed earth and put her head in her hands. She rubbed her eyes with the knuckles of her thumbs and tried to ignore the indignity of the few tears that escaped and made tracks down her cheeks. She picked up her head to see that the otter had come down off the perch and was now in front of her.

"I am sorry. I am in a hurry, but I should know better than to hurry a young human, even one who seems to hear so well as you. I will try better to explain." The otter began to walk around Elizabeth very slowly, staring down at the ground. "I am Gaia. I am the whole of the earth. Every living thing is a part of me and I am a part of it. Do you understand?"

Elizabeth thought of the picture of planet earth that was in her school books. "How can I be a part of the earth? I live on the earth."

"How can your nose be a part of you? It is on your face!"

"I move around on the earth!" Elizabeth retorted.

"Your snot runs down your nose!" The otter was still circling.

"But if I die, all my parts die too."

"Precisely!" The otter seemed relieved. "If I die, all my parts, including you, die too!"

Elizabeth shook her head as if to clear it. "I still don't get it."

"Let's talk about your little toe." The otter said. "Do you think about your little toe very much?"

"No."

"No you don't. And I know that you don't think about the parts that make up your toe. You probably have never stopped to consider the millions of cells that have lived and died inside your little toe; in those cells, mitochondria, enzymes and proteins, and deeper within, atoms: electrons, protons, neutrons. And it goes deeper still." The otter was still circling, and each time it passed Elizabeth, it paused to give her a good long stare. The otter paused in front of her. "Have you been thinking about four electrons in the fifth cell of your little toe? Do you need to talk to those four electrons to make them work?"

"No," Elizabeth whispered. She felt the beginning of understanding grow in the corner of her mind.

"Of course not! Your body is a pretty good system that continues to work as long as you give it healthy food and rest. But let us pretend for a moment that the fifth cell in your little toe went a little crazy." The otter resumed its slow circling, but now kept its eyes on Elizabeth.

"The fifth cell in the little toe starts to reproduce like mad. But the cells that it is reproducing are wrong. All the cells are now a tumor and you have cancer in your little toe. What would you do? Would you let the cancer spread until it killed you?"

"Are you calling people cancer?" Elizabeth exclaimed.

"I am saying that humans, who should be part of a system that runs very well, are going a little crazy like that cell. If something doesn't change soon, I will either have to kill all of you, or die. Either way, it is not good for you!"

"How can you die? You're a planet!" Elizabeth was getting angry. Nobody likes to be compared to cancer.

Again the otter stopped in front of her. Its eyes were flashing and its tail swished the dirt floor. "I breathe! I move! I feel pain and I love! I am not alone either. I think you understood my tale of the toe, because you have a toe. I will forgive you if you don't understand what I am about to say. I am one among many. We all move through the universe and talk and laugh and cry and share our stories. It is the same for us as it is for you. In the beginning there was nothing and then there was light."

Elizabeth jumped to her feet. "OK. So you think you are God? Am I supposed to start worshipping you now?"

The otter scampered back up onto the ledge and leveled its gaze at Elizabeth. "Absolutely not!" The voice had an edge like a distant rumble of thunder. "Granted, there have been many that have been able to hear me and a few that were able to speak to me. I have always tried to tell humans how to live so that you could stay healthy and I could stay healthy. When humans were new, they all listened.

But some humans thought they knew better. They started to listen to their own knowledge. Humans started making up their own systems for living and they moved away from me. They stopped listening, they stopped watching, and their hearts moved away from me. It is when they moved away from me that we started to pain each other.

I am no god. I live and I will die. Perhaps your little toe worships you, but you will die. I am just too young to die now! I cannot suffer humans much longer. I have spoken to you because I need your help, not because I want your praise!"

Elizabeth felt like her head was swimming. Thoughts of stars and toes and trees and animals and even her own family were swirling about her head. She got to her feet, closed her eyes, stamped her foot, and declared, "I just want to be at school."

She was roughly grabbed under her armpits and thrust up toward the ceiling. She scrunched her neck up expecting a blow to the head, but instead she was plunged into darkness and again she smelled the woody smell of trees and the moist damp of earth. Her body was bent and twisted about and her eyes and ears failed to tell her anything about what was happening.

She felt a sudden stop and her face pressed against bark until she thought she couldn't stand it. Then with a sudden release, she found herself standing under the large fir tree that stood in the center of the school's circular drive. She looked around quickly. A few kids who walked to school were starting to run because the bell was ringing. Elizabeth hesitated, then, she too ran to the front door of Avon Central School.

8
It Started Out Bad

Elizabeth jogged down the hall and turned left into her wing. The bell had stopped ringing and everyone was seated when she opened the classroom door. All heads turned her way. The outburst of laughter caught her off guard. Elizabeth was not only the kind of girl who was very careful about what she said, but was also careful about what she did and therefore had not often been the object of laughter. A few of her classmates were even pointing.

She looked to her left and saw in the mirror over the classroom sink that her face was streaked with dirt; bark and twigs were caught in her braids, her shirt collar was partially torn away and, because of the telltale streaks through the dirt, it was obvious she had been crying. She looked like the wobbly, scraggly little robin chick she and Rachel had found. It had fallen out of its nest. Elizabeth had spied the nest and Rachel had climbed up to put the chick back. Elizabeth wished someone could scoop her up and put her safely back into her nest of sheets and blankets at home.

Mrs. Foster took one look at Elizabeth and hurried to her side. "Elizabeth! Are you OK?" She grabbed a few paper towels and began to wipe at Elizabeth. She paused only long enough to wet the paper towels in the sink and tell the class, "Silence," and then returned to the job of cleaning Elizabeth's face. She was looking

Elizabeth up and down, probably looking for blood or protruding bones. "What happened to you?"

Elizabeth searched her mind for an explanation that wouldn't result in more questions. In her mind she heard a long, low chuckle and the sound of the wind jostling The Chaplain outside her window. She thought of the robin chick and came up with an answer. "I fell out of a tree."

Mrs. Foster sat back on her heels and furrowed her brow. "Was it one of the school's trees?"

"No."

"Do you think you need to go to the nurse?" Elizabeth shook her head.

"All right then, take your seat. You have all summer to climb trees. Try to stay out of them on school days."

As Elizabeth walked down the aisle to her seat, she caught Rachel's eye. Rachel looked away. When Elizabeth had sat down, Rachel leaned forward and whispered across the rows, "I can't believe you didn't call me last night! Some friend you are!"

Elizabeth turned around, shocked. After everything that had happened, how could Rachel be mad at her for not calling? *Because she doesn't know.* Elizabeth thought. *She knows that I know that she is moving, and she thinks I don't care. She doesn't know about the trees or the otter or anything.*

She opened her mouth to say something back to Rachel when Mrs. Foster called for everyone's attention. If there was one thing they had all learned in nine months of school with Mrs. Foster, it was that when she called for attention, you'd better give it to her!

Elizabeth sat and listened to the directions for field day, but only listened with half her mind. She was trying to think of what to tell Rachel. Should she tell her at all? Rachel was moving and she wouldn't be here to help Elizabeth figure out what was happening. Maybe Elizabeth could just pretend she had been sick and not say anything about the strange events of the past twenty-four hours.

"OK!" Mrs. Foster said brightly. "Pick your partners, get in line, and let's head out to the field." Elizabeth turned only to see Rachel stand up, cross the room, and grab Ruth Parker's hand. Ruth Parker? Seriously? Nobody really liked Ruth. She smelled funny and hummed to herself all the time. She was always the odd girl out. What was Rachel doing?

Suddenly Elizabeth realized that she was the only student not paired up. She felt a rising panic. Who would she run the two legged race with? Who would be her partner for the wheelbarrow? Mrs. Foster called to her, "Elizabeth, Mr. Clark also has an odd number of students. You'll be partnered with someone from his class."

Mr. Clark's class was the other fourth grade class, the one that Debbie Danner was in. To Elizabeth's horror, that was exactly who she was partnered up with. That meant that Debbie was the least liked girl in her class. She should have been partnered with Ruth. What was Rachel doing? Elizabeth felt a hint of her headache tapping behind her eyes.

"How come you weren't on the bus?" Debbie asked.

"I didn't feel good. I didn't think I could come to school, but then I changed my mind."

"That was stupid," Debbie said.

When they got out to the field, they stood along the sides to watch the first and second graders run a

50-yard dash. Elizabeth worked her way toward Rachel, but just when she reached out to tug her sleeve, Rachel gave her a quick sideways glance and said loudly to Ruth, "I'll be right back. I've got to go talk to a friend." Elizabeth felt relief wash over her. She could now explain and they would be partners. But to her confusion, Rachel turned away from her and walked downfield to begin talking to Becky Newman!

Elizabeth's sense of relief turned to anger. Fine! If Rachel didn't want to talk to her, she wouldn't even try. She went with the rest of the class to run their 50-yard dash. Elizabeth didn't come close to winning. Neither did Rachel. As always, Becky's best friend, Tracy Cox, blew the socks off all of them. Tracy might be a girly girl, but she could run wicked fast! Elizabeth always secretly admired her for that.

Elizabeth was absolutely miserable that morning. Her stomach complained about the lack of breakfast. Rachel still wasn't looking at her, much less speaking to her. To top it all off, once Dell Danner discovered Elizabeth in the three-legged race with his sister, he took every opportunity to jeer at them. Debbie was adept at ignoring Dell's meanness; but Elizabeth felt herself getting more and more frustrated and angry. By 11 a.m. she didn't know whether the knot in her stomach was from hunger or from dealing with Dell. Elizabeth was thinking that things couldn't possibly be any worse. She was wrong.

9
Then It Got Worse

It was the last race of the morning, the wheelbarrow race, when it happened. Elizabeth was the wheelbarrow, so she was walking on her hands while Debbie Danner carried her legs. They were actually doing pretty well. Elizabeth started to get excited when she saw Becky Newman and Tracy Cox fall down. There was no one ahead of them! They were going to win! Elizabeth was just starting to smile when Dell Danner stepped out from the spectators on their right.

Elizabeth saw his grubby sneakers and knew what was about to happen. His left foot shot out and tripped his sister. As she fell, she pushed Elizabeth forward so hard and fast that Elizabeth's arms buckled and she found her chin, mouth and nose being driven into the dirt. As Debbie Danner came crashing down on top of her, she could hear Dell laughing the 'ha-ha' laugh that every bully seems to master by grade three.

Elizabeth spit grass out of her mouth and started to push up on her forearms. Dell Danner squatted down, grinning and shaking his head. "Boy, you guys are a couple of real losers!"

He stood up, turned his back to Elizabeth and continued to laugh loudly. Elizabeth, still spitting grass out of her mouth and blowing dirt out of her nose was beyond mad. She was furious. As soon as Debbie rolled off her, she jumped to her feet and yelled. "Hey Dell!

Have a nice trip!"

She didn't know how she did it. But she knew that she could do it. She knew she could do it and didn't care that she really didn't know what "it" was. All her anger and humiliation and frustration from the morning drained down her body, through her feet, and into the ground.

The grass humped up about three inches and began to move like a wave toward Dell. It looked much like it does when you give a throw rug a shake and a snap. Dell was looking back over his shoulder at Elizabeth and not the ground. He didn't see the wave of Elizabeth's anger coming towards his feet at a rapid pace. Dell had been planning on calling out a nice long "Loooooooooooser!" He got as far as "Loo," when the rolling rise of soil lifted him up and dumped him on his rear end.

The kids around Dell began to laugh. Everyone enjoys it when the tables turn on the class bully. Elizabeth didn't laugh. Her eyes were on the ground and something horrifying was happening.

Dell began to yell. It was the kind of yell people give

when they realize they have a bee or a leech on them. He cried, "Get it off! Get it off!" But he didn't lift his hands to brush at anything. Elizabeth realized that the soil around Dell was lifting up and over him! He appeared to be sinking into the ground. When his left foot disappeared under the grass he really started to howl.

Mr. Toski, Dell's teacher, pushed through the crowd of children, grabbed Dell by his shirt collar, and pulled him roughly to his feet. Dirt flew and there was a five foot-long trench of bare earth where Dell had been. Elizabeth could see that the dirt was sliding and swirling.

"Mr. Danner!" Mr. T shouted. "What have I told you about school property? Go to the office and explain to Mr. Brown why you decided to dig a hole in our field!" Dell whimpered and tried to say something coherent in his defense. But Dell's teachers learned pretty quickly that Dell was a perpetrator, not a victim. Mr. T turned Dell around and gave him a little shove between the shoulder blades. "And you can stay at the office for the remainder of the day."

While everyone's attention had been on Mr. T and Dell, Elizabeth had kept her eyes on the ground. The dirt was still sifting and moving. At the base of the trench, a small crack opened in the grass. Like a finger it began to creep outward toward Elizabeth. It was then that she remembered what Gaia had said about getting her feet off the ground. She ran toward the school and in through the side entrance of the gymnasium.

Once inside, her head exploded back into the rhythmic throbbing that she had felt that morning. She staggered across the gym floor and pushed through the double doors into the hall. She had to put one hand across her eyes because the light from the window felt like it was beating her eyes into her skull. With her other hand on the wall for guidance, she went down the long hall toward the office.

Elizabeth entered the main office. She could hear Dell's whining, pleading voice behind the closed door of the principal. She moved quickly past the main desk and into the nurse's office. "I don't feel good," she said, and then for the second time that day, her vision narrowed and everything went black.

When she woke up, she was on one of the narrow cots, a cold washcloth across her forehead. She could hear the nurse on the phone and knew that it was her mother on the other end.

"Mrs. Angier, are you sure you don't want us to call an ambulance. The child did pass out! No. No. No blood. She has a lot of dirt on her face. I am assuming this was a field day mishap. OK. OK. OK, Mrs. Angier. We will see you shortly."

The nurse hung up and pulled her sizable bulk up out of the desk chair. The chair squeaked with relief. She crossed the room to Elizabeth and bent over her. Elizabeth opened one eye. "Elizabeth?" the nurse said. "I can see you're awake. Lie still. I'm going to get you some apple juice. Your mother will be here in a few minutes."

The nurse came back with a paper cup and a straw. She put the straw in the corner of Elizabeth's mouth. "Drink." Elizabeth pulled the apple juice up through the straw. The cold sweetness filled her mouth and cooled her throat. Elizabeth thought it was the best apple juice she had ever tasted.

The nurse took the cup over to her desk and came back with a clipboard and a pen. "Elizabeth, I need to fill out some paperwork. Tell me what happened."

For the second time that day, she was searching her mind for an explanation that would not lead to more questions. She couldn't use the falling out of the tree story. There were no trees on the field where field day was taking place.

"I fell. I was the wheelbarrow and I fell on my chin. I'm also hungry and thirsty. I didn't eat this morning."

"Ahhh!" The nurse said and nodded her head with understanding. "That would explain the fainting. Your blood sugar is probably quite low; it is ridiculous to skip breakfast and then race around a hot field. You should know better!" She jotted a few more things down and asked if Elizabeth wanted to sit up and have some more juice.

By the time Elizabeth's mother came in, her headache was receding like a bad dream. Mrs. Foster came hurrying in. "Oh thank God!" she said when she saw Elizabeth on the cot. "Elizabeth! You know you don't leave the group without permission! Hello Mrs. Angier, I hope you know I looked Elizabeth over very carefully. I didn't see her fall from the tree. It wasn't on school property and Elizabeth assured me she was fine."

The nurse swiveled toward her. "Tree? I thought you said it was the wheelbarrow race." They all looked down at her. Elizabeth looked down at the blanket.

"It was both. I mean... I was in a tree this morning, but I fell in the race too." She didn't dare look up.

Much to Elizabeth's relief, no one pressed her further. Her mother began to mutter, "Honestly Elizabeth, how many times have I told you only to climb in the backyard." She turned to the other two women. "This child is crazy for trees. I was pulling her out of poplars before she was out of Pampers!" They all laughed that knowing-parent laugh.

Elizabeth swung her feet to the floor and stood up. There was a moment when her vision felt a little prickly, but it cleared up and she left the office with her mother.

Her mother held her hand as they crossed the

parking lot. She was muttering something about letting her skip breakfast. Once they were in the car, she turned to Elizabeth and said, "This was your last day of school with Rachel. How is she?"

"I didn't talk to her much." Elizabeth said. She felt a dark blue sadness in the pit of her stomach. "Well, she didn't talk to me much. I think she's mad at me and I'm not sure why."

Elizabeth's mother smiled. "Honey, sometimes when people have to leave the ones they love, they make it easier for themselves by getting mad first. It is easier to say goodbye if you're mad, rather than sad."

"I guess." Elizabeth didn't quite understand what her mother was saying. All she knew was that it was the last day of school. She should be happy and excited about the beginning of summer vacation. Instead, her best friend was mad at her, her parents were having secret talks about selling her farm, and she had become the object of attention to a talking otter. She leaned her head against the window and sighed. It was going to be a long summer.

10
Sing Song Creek

Elizabeth had the kind of mother who knew when to scold or pry or just be quiet and supportive. Elizabeth was profoundly grateful for that fact when they got home and her mother didn't ask her a lot of questions. Instead, they went into the kitchen and her mother made her a big bowl of strawberries and cream. The strawberries were from their own green-house and the cream came from the Jeffries'dairy. The two tastes mingled together and seemed to combine all the good things from the two farms.

Her mother leaned against the counter and watched her spoon up her strawberries and cream. She finally said, "Well, Elizabeth, you're dirty beyond all redemption. I would send you to the bath, except I just cleaned it. What do you think about taking some soap down to the creek?"

Elizabeth didn't hesitate. She pushed back her chair and walked over to hug her mom.

She left her mother picking radishes in the garden and Maizey snoring in the shade of the garden shed. She headed down the slope behind the barn. There was a wonderful shaded path that ran parallel to Sing Song Creek. Her father often remarked that many genera-tions and more than a few Indians had used this path. Elizabeth knew that she had some Indian blood in her. At school they had been taught to use the phrase

'Native American,' but Elizabeth preferred Indian, since that is what her dad said, and that is what he said her grandfather and great grandfather had said, and it was her great grandfather's own mother who had been the Indian in the family!

When Elizabeth was six, she had asked what kind of Indian she was (partly, anyway). Her father grinned his jokester grin and said, "Well, Little Lizbeth, I do believe you are part Blackfoot!" Elizabeth had been immensely proud about that. She had thought on it and turned the word over in her mind and imagined what kind of tribe the Blackfoot were. At school she found a book in the library and was stunned but excited to see the pictures of the dark, fierce-looking men with their hair in braids and the groups of teepees on the wide prairies. She hadn't stopped to wonder how it was she was related to a tribe that was so far to the west.

It was a year later when they were in the Fredricks' Hardware Store that Elizabeth found out the truth behind her father's answer. She had gone with her father to buy a new axe handle. She loved the hardware store; it always seemed full of possibilities. While he selected a handle, Elizabeth spied the hatchets. They reminded her of the tomahawks the Blackfoot Indians used. She carried one up to the front counter where her father was talking to Marv Hollings, Mr. Fredrick, and a tall man Elizabeth didn't know.

"Look dad! It's like a tomahawk!" She then turned to Mr. Fredrick and said, "I'm part Blackfoot Indian, you know."

Mr. Fredrick turned to her father. "I thought you were part Iroquois; Seneca, wasn't it?"

Her father looked down at her and started to say, "Elizabeth, you know you're part Seneca, why do you think..." He paused and then he started to laugh. The other men smiled, not getting the joke. He squatted down, still grinning. "I told you that you were Blackfoot because at the time you asked me you had been running around barefoot all day and your feet were really dirty! Blackfoot! Get it!" He stood and started to relay the story to the other men. She had stood there and had felt like a small, silly girl.

As she had walked back down the dim aisle to

replace the hatchet, she heard the front of the store fill with big grown-up laughter. They got the joke. Elizabeth hated it when people laughed at her expense. She had been quiet in the truck all the way home.

When her father parked out back by the greenhouse, she had turned to get out. "Wait, Elizabeth."

She sat facing the truck's window. She was still mad about those men laughing at her.

"I can tell you're mad at me, so I'm apologizing. What I am curious about is: are you mad because of the joke, or are you mad because you aren't Blackfoot?"

Elizabeth had continued to look at the truck's door. "Both, I guess. I looked up the Blackfoot and they seemed really wild. I thought it was cool."

Her father chuckled. "Being Seneca is pretty cool too. Don't ever forget that our ancestors are the true Americans. Your relations were walking these hills and fishing in these creeks before anybody else. I think that's cool."

She had turned to look at him and couldn't resist smiling along with the grin that stretched his face. "Me too. So, we're cool."

Now, Elizabeth turned right to walk westward. It was to the west that the best swimming hole was. It was deep and shaded and cool. Of course, this early in the summer, all of Sing Song Creek was cool enough to take your breath away for a moment. Elizabeth didn't care. She loved to swim and splash in the water and always started and ended the swimming season in quite cool water.

As she walked under the shade of the weeping willows, she began to feel better. Insects were buzzing in the tall grass of the uncut hayfields that were just on the other side of the trees and bushes lining the creek. She heard the high, short call of a red-tailed hawk. She began to feel that maybe all that had transpired was a bad dream. She knew that it wasn't, but at least at this moment, life was fine.

She began to whistle in a way that complemented the swallows and the robins and even the rude cry of the blue jays. The willows hummed their own tune in concert with the rising breeze. She decided to take off her sneakers and leave them beside the path. After all, this was still their property and the odds of anyone else coming down the creekside path were slim.

Her bare feet met the cool packed earth of the path and her heart was lifted even more. She knew that she could make things right with Rachel. After all, they had been friends since kindergarten and had talked about so many things, that maybe a talking otter might not seem so weird. *It's like the Chronicles of Narnia,* Elizabeth thought. That is what she would tell Rachel. They both loved the series of books that featured a host of talking creatures as characters.

Don't forget, Rachel's leaving. She's probably more scared than I am. Elizabeth thought. *She is going to a strange place. She probably won't be able to go to a swimming hole, eat sugar snap peas right off the plant or have fresh strawberries and cream.* That last thought made Elizabeth feel profoundly selfish. Although the last twenty-four hours had been scary and confusing, she still knew that tonight she would be home in her own bed. Most likely, this time next year, she would be home in her bed. *Unless we have to sell the farm,* her mind offered. She pushed that thought aside and hurried down the path.

Elizabeth was rinsing off the last of the soap when she was practically jolted right out of the water. "Hey there, Lizard Breath!" Elizabeth looked up on the bank and there was Will. He was still in his school clothes. "Your mom sent me down to make sure you were OK. You look OK. What happened today?"

Elizabeth pulled herself up out of the swimming hole using the roots of the willow tree that shaded the creek at this bend. She brushed her wet hair off her face and said, nonchalantly she hoped, "What do you mean? Nothing happened."

"You weren't on the bus, but Dell and Debbie were talking about you all the way home. Something about you getting in trouble at field day?"

"I'm not the one who got in trouble. As always, that was Dell." Even as she said this, she felt a pang of guilt because she knew that technically, Dell didn't get in trouble for what he should have gotten in trouble for, which was tripping her and Debbie.

"Well anyway," Will continued, "You weren't on the bus and I thought you weren't even at school. I was surprised your mom let you go swimming. Do you need anything?"

"Will," Elizabeth began, imitating her mother's exasperated voice, "what could I possibly need? Don't you have work to do?"

"Yeah, smarty pants, your mom is paying me ten bucks to do all your chores. Have fun swimming."

He turned and headed up the path. Elizabeth, being the kind of girl who didn't speak unless she knew exactly what she was going to say, didn't say anything. She simply watched his back retreating down the path and when he disappeared around a small curve, she sat her wet bottom down on the grassy bank and leaned against the willow tree.

Why am I making all my friends mad at me? she thought. *What is wrong with me?*

A voice came that sounded like a hundred song birds, all in harmony and rhythm. "There is nothing wrong with you, my dear. Actually, everything about you is right. That is why I chose you as one of the four. You are the first of the four. You are earth."

11
If You Are Ready

"You!" Elizabeth cried as she jumped to her feet. She planted her hands on her hips, narrowed her eyes, and looked down on the sleek, wet otter that was standing on its hind legs with its paws on its hips, staring right back at her. "I almost got in trouble because of you! Rachel is mad at me because of you! I don't have anything to say to you!" Elizabeth made a show of turning her back and gathering up her soap and towel and dry tee-shirt.

"Listen, dear heart, do you think this is easy or fun for me? I am the one who is sick and dying. I am the one who has spent a millennium trying to figure out a way to communicate with you humans. I am the one who is putting my faith in a ten-year-old. And, I might add, one that doesn't seem to know how to wash behind her ears!"

Elizabeth couldn't help but scrub one finger behind her right ear. "You're an otter. You are just a river otter and I've been so upset that I'm hearing things. You don't need me. Go be an otter and leave me alone!"

The otter dropped to all fours and laughed a laugh that sounded like broken glass rolling down a metal chute. "You think I am just an otter, eh?"

Elizabeth felt nervous that the musical quality of the otter's voice was changing. "I was hoping you would grasp all this sooner;" its voice grew so low that it almost sounded like far-off thunder. "If you cannot grasp me this way, I will grasp you another!"

Before Elizabeth's eyes, the otter turned to fine sand and fell into the hard pack of the path. The path humped up, much like the grass in the school's field earlier that day. The bump of earth began to roll toward Elizabeth. She jumped to her left and the hump of dirt hit the base of the willow.

A shimmer rolled up the trunk of the willow and the branches began to shake wildly, as if a strong wind were swirling around it. Two long branches reached down and scooped Elizabeth up. Elizabeth opened her mouth to yell, but nothing came out. She was raised high into the air and then dumped with a splash into the deepest part of the swimming hole.

Elizabeth kicked to the surface. She spun about to get her bearings. On the shore the otter was waving one paw. It then flopped down in the dirt and rolled about, laughing a laugh that sounded like a concert of flutes.

Elizabeth stroked over to the creek's bank. "Stop laughing!" she demanded. "Stop laughing and start explaining what you want." Elizabeth stood in waist-deep water and waited for the otter's response.

The otter finally rolled to all four paws. "You should have seen your face as you flew through the air! Priceless!" The otter uttered a few more giggles and then tucked its paws under and slid neatly down the bank and into the creek with hardly a splash.

The otter surfaced next to Elizabeth and said, "If you are finally ready to get down to business, I suggest you follow me." The otter swam back towards the bank. Then, much to Elizabeth's amazement, underneath the willow's roots, a crack opened in the bank and they swam right in.

The water became shallower until Elizabeth was wading. Soon, she and the otter were walking on wet earth. It was damp and cool and smelled pleasant. They turned left and up ahead, light could be seen streaming down from above. The otter pulled up through the small opening without a hitch, but Elizabeth could see that she wouldn't be able to fit through. The otter's pointed snout poked back down through the hole.

"Aren't you coming?"

"In case you hadn't noticed, I'm a little bigger than you are."

"Lesson number one: Sink your toes into the dirt and ask."

Elizabeth was about to launch into a question, but decided to -- as the otter put it -- get down to business. She wiggled her toes a little deeper into the soft soil and said out loud, "Open Sesame." She looked up at the hole and the otter expectantly.

"What do you think this is," the otter asked, "a movie? Ask the hole to open wider and let you through. Better yet, close your eyes, see the hole growing bigger and then ask."

Elizabeth closed her eyes and imagined what the hole would look like as it opened. She then thought, *Please open.* Much to her delight, the dirt sifted and fell about her feet until it was just as she had imagined it.

"Good girl! I knew I chose wisely! Come! Come! Let's get to work!"

Elizabeth didn't hesitate. She set off down the

shaded path after the otter. She couldn't resist calling ahead to the shiny, round otter rear, "I've got questions, ya know!"

"I've got answers, ya know!" Gaia called back. Elizabeth smiled. Maybe a talking otter wasn't such a bad thing.

12
I am Gaia II

When the path came to an end, Elizabeth stopped with her mouth opened. There before her was something from her dreams. The woods opened out into the shape of a perfect circle. The grass inside the circle was like a soft lawn. There was a ring of trembling aspens marking the perimeter and in the center was a large rock. Around the rock were concentric rings of small yellow buttercups and fragrant blue violets.

"A fairy ring!" Elizabeth whispered. She was awestruck. Her mother used to tell her stories of fairy rings in the woods. These were the places, her mother had said, that wood fairies and elves would hold their moonlight meetings. It captured her imagination as a small child and, even though she was now ten and too old to believe in fairies, she still had a secret wish to see a fairy ring.

And here it was. Gaia scampered ahead and climbed up on the rock. "Come and sit and we will talk. I know you have questions and I will allow you to ask three. Then we will get on with our business."

Elizabeth walked across the lawn and settled cross-legged in the second ring of violets. She looked about trying to get a glimpse of the hilltops in order to get her bearings and know where she was. "Where is this?" she finally asked. "Is it on our farm?"

"I made this place just for you and just for today."

"How?"

"Are you sure you want that to be your second question?"

Elizabeth hadn't thought of it as her second question. So she picked a violet and twirled it between her thumb and forefinger while she thought of a better question.

"Did I make the ground at school knock over Dell Danner?"

"Yes."

Elizabeth kept looking up, but was disappointed when Gaia didn't elaborate. She looked back down at the violet in her hand.

"Are there other people that can hear you too?"

"Yes. And that is an excellent question to begin with. Get comfortable, I am going to explain again who I am and what I am asking you to do. Try to hold your questions until I give you leave to ask."

Elizabeth tucked the violet behind her ear, set her elbows on her knees and her chin in her hands. "Hit it."

Much like she did that morning, Gaia began to walk in a slow circle, looking down as she spoke. Elizabeth decided that if she closed her eyes she would be able to pay better attention to what Gaia was saying.

"As I said before, I am Gaia. I am the whole of the earth. As a whole being, I breathe, I move, I rest, I live. I will also die, but I am hoping that will not happen too soon. Remember what I told you about your little toe?"

Elizabeth looked down at her own muddy pinky toe. She thought for a moment about all the cells in that toe and how she never had to think about them for them to work. "Yes."

"OK. So, and please do not be insulted by this, but you are like one electron in one cell in my little toe. I know people think that because they can think, that means they must be the most important thing. However, all the creatures of the earth, plants and bugs included are essential to making it work.

Just like you need your lungs as much as you need your heart, I need my oceans as much as I need the beetles that help decompose the trees that fall. It all works together."

Elizabeth interjected, "My father and mother taught me that too! I have seen it on Tree T. V. and then when we dump our dinner leavings into the compost bin, it does the same kind of thing. We dump the compost on the baby trees. The baby trees grow up and give us more shade and oxygen, right?"

Gaia paused in her circling. "You were born with a gift, and you also had the great good fortune to be born to people who knew that this world is meant to live in a balance. I first heard you when you were just a little thing walking up and down your garden rows thanking the earthworms for making the dirt that fed the blackcaps that you love so much.

Elizabeth, people have always used my water, and eaten the creatures that roam upon me, and that was all well and good and balanced. But something is changing."

Elizabeth waited patiently for Gaia to continue. The otter stared at the ground and when she turned her eyes toward Elizabeth, there were great tears trembling in the corners of them.

"Grave things are happening: things I have never before felt. The water deep in my belly is being drained faster than it returns. My mountaintops are being shorn off and great tears in my flesh are being made. Rivers have been made to stop flowing to the sea and the sky is filled with foulness. It hurts! I have tried to shake off such pains and have only killed thousands of innocents."

"What do you mean?" Elizabeth was feeling scared again.

"There is only so much I can do. I shake, but these new pains do not go away. The holes do not go away. The sky does not clear. I only feel the added pain of 5,000 people dying. I know these are not the people drilling because the drilling does not stop. Everything I have tried -- flood, fire, famine -- has only hurt those who are doing me no harm. I have struggled to find a way to be more precise. I need to save myself without destroying more of you!"

"How can I help?" Elizabeth felt close to tears. She felt sorry for Gaia. She felt bad for all the people that had died in earthquakes and floods and fires.

Gaia rolled onto her otter back and closed her deep brown eyes. She lay like that for a while, her otter belly going up and down with deep breath. Elizabeth began to wonder if she had gone to sleep.

"I have not gone to sleep," Gaia said. Elizabeth, again, was startled. How did Gaia know? "I am enjoying the feeling of this belly fur being warmed by the sun. It is so different than the sunshine on my mountain peaks or the sun that warms the southern ocean waves: different, but just as pleasurable."

Gaia rolled back to her paws. She walked over and put her front paws on Elizabeth's knees and rose up until they were nose to nose. Elizabeth thought she should be scared, but the truth was, she wasn't. She could feel the otter breath against her nose and see the reflection of her own face, dirty and streaked again, reflected in Gaia's big brown eyes.

"You can be much more precise than I can. Now that I know you can hear me, now that I know you can adopt some of my power, we can, together, redirect or remove the ones that hurt me most. You are one of four. You are the earth and to you I give the power over soil, rock and mountain top. You will be able to work with the creatures that reside within the soil. Bugs and bunnies, woodchucks and weasels will listen when you call. Earthworms and echidnas will respond to your will. (Elizabeth wasn't sure what an echidna was, but she trembled at the thought of these powers.) As you have discovered already, you are able not only to hear the trees, but also to talk to them and to ask them for help. Listen, and let us begin your lessons."

Gaia balanced on her back legs and reached out her wee paws to draw Elizabeth's eyelids closed. "Listen," Gaia said, and the word sounded like a symphony of bells.

13
A Wild Ride

Elizabeth took a deep breath and focused on the bell-like echo of Gaia's words. *Listen, listen, listen,"* the echo said. Elizabeth sat with her eyes closed and began to feel a slight sway in her body. The swaying she felt was soon accompanied by lilting music. The tune was light and breezy and somehow funny. She began to smile. "Open your eyes," she heard Gaia say.

She opened her eyes and all around her the trembling aspens that made up the fairy ring were swaying to and fro in unison. Elizabeth was swaying right along with them! Their spinning, sparkling leaves seemed to be giggling. The trees were laughing and singing, and although her ears were filled with music, words that she could understand somehow came forth. *Welcome! Welcome! Lover of trees, ask to come up and be sure to say please.* The trees swayed and the music seemed to move from the tips of their leaves down to their roots and through the ground to her. Elizabeth started to laugh and laugh. She waited for the right moment in the wild green music and sang out, "Please!"

The aspen directly in front of her bent forward at a frightful angle that would normally break its trunk in two. Two large branches scooped Elizabeth up from the ground and she found herself held high above the fairy ring. For a brief moment she was scared of falling. But she quickly realized that unlike when she climbed a tree, she didn't have to hold herself fixed to the branches. The tree alone was holding her and she was safe to sway to and fro and be part of the wild green song.

It was better than any ride she had been on at the county fair. Elizabeth laughed a wild laugh and she flew left and right. She was suddenly reminded of being very small, a toddler, and having her father toss her high in the air. It felt like that. Children don't worry about their father dropping them and Elizabeth didn't worry about this beautiful aspen dropping her now.

Into the song she heard a high voice call, *My turn! My turn!* Elizabeth's breath caught as the tree that held her pulled back and then with a mighty whipping motion, threw her in a high arch across the fairy ring. She let out a long squeal as she flew. She could see Gaia's pointy otter head looking up at her as she passed overhead. The aspen across the ring caught her neatly in its boughs and Elizabeth dissolved into laughter of relief.

All the trees seemed to be laughing with her. She

finally gasped, "Put me down, please." And the aspen bowed forward and put her neatly down. She rolled onto her back, turned her face to the sun and caught her breath. The music of the trees began to fade and when she opened her eyes the trees were still as could be, just the tremble of their leaves revealing the wind's direction.

Elizabeth rolled to her belly and pushed herself up. She walked on wobbly legs to the center of the ring and perched on the rock. Her hands were shaking, but she couldn't stop smiling. Gaia came to her in that strange otter humping gait. "Well?" Gaia asked.

Elizabeth stared at Gaia for a moment. She finally said, "Thank you, Gaia! That was wonderful! Somehow I always knew, but I didn't really know, ya know?"

Gaia laughed a laugh that sounded like moonlight sparkling on water. "I think many people sort of know. Not many are lucky to grow up in such a green place and have the peace to listen as closely as you have. Now, close your eyes and think of the oak in your backyard; tell me what you see or hear."

Elizabeth took a deep breath and in her mind

pictured The Chaplain. She thought of the pattern of shadow that it cast upon the house. She thought of the strong branch that held the swing. It was then that she heard quite clearly her mother's voice. "Elizzzzzabeeettthhh!" Then she heard the big school bell clanging.

Elizabeth's eyes flew open. At her house, the clanging bell meant it was time to be in for supper! "Gaia! I'm late! I'm gonna get in trouble!"

"Shhhh. Think of the oak again. Ask permission of the earth and the roots and all the creatures for safe passage. Put your feet onto the ground and send your request into the roots of the earth. You will be home before you know it."

Elizabeth closed her eyes and again thought of her backyard oak. She took a deep breath in and thought, *May I please pass through all the roots and dirt and passages to The Chaplain in the backyard.* She felt the question travel from her mind to her toes. She felt a slight shaking and opened her eyes in time to see the ground beneath her feet open wide and for the third time that day, she was plunged into darkness.

She felt the bending, twisting and rending of her body. Her eyes and ears and nose were full and she had no thought as to where she was or what was happening. She heard the clanging of a bell getting closer. She felt a quick rising up and then, to her astonishment, she was in the oak in her backyard.

Below, her mother was swinging the old school bell back and forth. The deep clang was a sound that Elizabeth knew well and it made her smile. Her mother cupped her hand to her mouth and called again, "Elllizzzzzzabeeetttttthhhhh!"

"I'm here," Elizabeth called down. Her mother jumped. She gazed up into the green of the tree. Elizabeth almost laughed to see her mother's eyes and mouth opened wide in surprise.

Her mother quickly closed her mouth and recovered her motherly composure by saying, "Elizabeth Angier, come down here. Look at you! You are dirtier than when I sent you to the creek! I think you have climbed enough trees for one day! Where are your shoes?"

Elizabeth began to climb down. She had never

climbed so high in this tree before and realized that she wasn't sure of the path down. She heard a low chuckle and the branch below her left foot bent itself to accommodate Elizabeth's descent. "Thank you!" Elizabeth whispered, and patted the trunk with appreciation. She swung from the lowest branch and landed in the cool grass of the backyard.

14
Counting Sheep

Elizabeth ran to the upstairs bathroom and was surprised to see that she looked much like she did when she staggered into Mrs. Foster's classroom that morning. Her hair was snarled and carried a few twigs and leaves. Her face was streaked with dirt and grime. However, unlike the scared baby bird feeling of the morning, a big smile now tugged at her cheeks. Her heart felt light and a laugh was just below the surface waiting to pop out.

Another long summer twilight was beginning when they all sat down at the table on the big screened-in back porch. The rolling hills to the west were still rimmed with golden sunlight, although the sun had sunk from view ten minutes prior. At supper, she was surprised when her father asked her how she felt.

"I feel great!" Elizabeth blurted before she remembered that she had almost stayed home from school and had been picked up from the nurse's office earlier that very day. Her father looked at her side-eyed and a grin played at the corner of his mouth.

"Ready for summer I take it?" he asked. Elizabeth looked down at her chicken and potatoes. What could she say? *Well, I was tossed about by a stand of aspens and it made my headache go away.*

Her mother saved her the trouble by interjecting. Her voice was flat and matter of fact. "I spoke with

Rachel's mother today. It seems that everything is a done deal. She is leaving with Rachel in three days and Rachel's dad will follow them in a week or two when everything has been signed over and the movers can come. I guess there is an apartment waiting for them in Florida."

The grin her dad had held for Elizabeth faded and his brows knitted together, making a big crease between his eyes. He stared down at his plate and twirled his fork in his potatoes. "Marv Hollings stopped today. Seems he is selling as well." Her mother's eyes grew wide. "And that's not all," her father continued, "the rep from Harmony Farms is over at the Danner place right now."

He set down his fork and sighed. Her mother was holding her hand over her mouth and her eyes were even wider. Elizabeth looked back and forth between them, waiting for one of them to say the kind of things that grownups do to make you feel less scared. But they didn't. Her father continued to stare down at the plate. Her mother stood up stiffly and began to clear the table even though the food wasn't half gone.

The Danners are right next door! What does that mean? What does a rep do, anyway? Could he make us sell Three Oaks? Elizabeth's mind was a flurry of questions. But, being the kind of girl who didn't like to speak unless she knew exactly what she was going to say, she decided to let one of her parents speak first. She sat and waited and felt small and scared. The day had been a roller coaster of emotion and she was starting to feel drained.

She watched her father and waited. She could hear the quick chirp of a chipmunk, sounding the alarm to his chipmunk friends. She listened to the chattering blackbirds having a raucous meeting, probably about how to best pull up the corn seedlings. She waited and heard the sighing of The Chaplain's leaves. They too, seemed to be waiting.

He finally looked up at her and smiled a weak smile that had no fun in it. "Elizabeth, run and do your chores and then come to my office." She was about to ask him why, but he stood up, put his cap back on, and headed out to the barn. Maizey watched him go and began to whine a little bit in the back of her throat.

Elizabeth knelt down and wrapped her arms around the big dog. "It's OK, Maizey. Everything is going to be OK." Maizey thumped her tail against the table leg and pushed her big wet nose against Elizabeth's cheek. "I know, I know, chores. Wanna look for rabbits?" The word rabbits inspired Maizey, although the rabbits always outsmarted the big dog by doubling back on their own tracks and holding still in the underbrush. But that didn't seem to dampen Maizey's enthusiasm; she bounded out the back door and down the slope toward the barn. Elizabeth followed and went down to the tree nursery.

She paused at the spigot and sighed. She was so tired she felt she couldn't possibly water all the saplings. She thought of the aspens in the fairy ring and had an inspiration. She closed her eyes, took a deep breath and thought, *Who is so very, very thirsty that they can't wait until tomorrow? Please wave your branches.* She exhaled and felt the thought travel down her body and into her feet. A breeze seemed to move through the branches of saplings and Elizabeth heard a high, thin music that carried the hint of small voices. *He came. The tall one watered. He was here for you today. That tall one.* A grin spread across Elizabeth's face. She had forgotten that Will had done her biggest chore for her.

She left the nursery and continued down the slope to the bridge that crossed Sing Song Creek. She paused on the bridge, as always, to gaze downstream. She loved the way the willows arched over the water and tonight the fading sunlight was filtering through the lattice of the leaves, accentuating their drape and pattern. She watched the willows dip and sway in the gentle evening breeze and made a mental note to come and visit the willows soon. She was interested to know what kind of song they might sing. Would it be the same as the aspens? Could all the trees sing, or just certain ones? She wondered when she would see Gaia again.

She continued over the bridge and could see the silhouettes of the sheep dotted up the slope of the pasture, their shadows laid out long behind them. She moved her mouth and silently counted them: forty-seven. She turned and headed back toward the house.

The twilight was deepening and the world was layered with shades of deep blue. A few fireflies began to send out their blinking lights, their flickering love notes. Robins and wrens chattered as they hurried to find their place to roost for the night and far off in the west she could hear the cry of the sea birds that had come to vacation on the Avon River.

Elizabeth heard the rumbling of the big barn door sliding in its track. She watched the dark form of her father slide the latch home. He began to walk toward the house. Elizabeth noticed his head was tilted down, watching his feet. This made her stomach feel tight. It meant he was worried. An early summer evening as fine as this one would normally have her father's eyes and nose and ears up and casting about, looking for wildlife, sniffing the wind for rain, and admiring the hues of the twilight.

She ran up behind him and grabbed his hand. He jumped, surprised, and smiled down at her, a real smile this time. "Hey there! Did you count 'em all?" he said, referring to the sheep.

"Yes sir, forty-seven."

"How 'bout their legs?" He was now looking at her with his joking grin on his face.

"Daddy!" Elizabeth said and punched him in the arm. It was an old joke. When Elizabeth had been too little to count the sheep, her father used to walk her down to the pasture each night and ask her to look close for any lopsided sheep.

"You know, sheep that graze on a hillside like this can end up with one set of legs shorter than the other," he had said. He had what some might take to be a serious look on his face, but as Elizabeth grew to know, the jokester grin fought to surface and made the dimples in his cheeks a little deeper.

"Look close, Little Lizbeth. Let me know if I need to turn them around tomorrow and face them the other way."

Elizabeth still remembers the moment when the joke was revealed to her. Cousin Nick, who was her father's cousin, not hers, had come to visit. At dinner the first night he had asked Elizabeth what she did to help on the farm. She sat up proudly and said, "I help Momma water the garden, I feed Maizey, and I make extra sure the sheeps' legs stay even."

The table had erupted with laughter. Her father and Cousin Nick had rocked back in their chairs and laughed until tears came out of their eyes. It turned out that her grandfather had played the same joke on her father. Elizabeth had wanted to feel mad, but in her heart, she was proud that her father would treat her the same as his father had treated him.

The entire memory flashed through her mind in the time that it took her to punch his arm. He squeezed her shoulder and said, "Come in my office; I have something for you."

15
Be Brave

Elizabeth loved going into the office because most of the time she was kept out. The exceptions were Sunday afternoon and Wednesday night. That's when her mother would let her use the computer. She would read about things like polar bears and dolphins. Sometimes she'd search for things she had to write about at school. She would wait for Rachel to get online. When she saw her Instant Message name, HorsiGrl, she would send her a message and they would chat. Elizabeth's IM name was GardnGrl. She always felt bad that she actually had a garden and Rachel never did get a horse! Sometimes she would send an e-mail to her Aunt Felicia, her mother's sister in New York City.

Aunt Felicia didn't like being out in the country. Whenever they saw her in the city, she would roll her eyes and say something like, "Honestly, Julia, I don't know how you keep from dying of boredom out there in the sticks." Her mother usually just smiled an inward, knowing kind of smile and said something like, "Each to their own!" Elizabeth always wondered why her mother didn't explain all the wonderful things there were to do and see on their farm. She wished her mother would take her wonderful journal to show her.

Elizabeth's mother had a spiral-bound book that she sketched in. In it were all the treasures of Three

Oaks. There were drawings of all the birds that filled their world with music. There was a sketch of the salamander that Elizabeth had found at one of her Tree T.V. sites. She had wanted to keep the strange orange creature, but her mother said it was easier to keep it by drawing it instead. There were sketches of the oaks and the creek and the garden rows. There were sketches of herbs and wildflowers and butterflies. Elizabeth knew her mother was happy when she saw her on her folding stool, humming and drawing.

All that probably didn't matter to Aunt Felicia. She usually liked to talk about shoes and sales and shows. When she had come to visit Three Oaks, she kept looking around nervously and asking about bears. Elizabeth loved Aunt Felicia, but didn't really understand her.

Now, she sat on the old leather sofa and looked around. A spider fern hung in the corner, dangling its baby spider ferns down over the file cabinets. In the left hand corner was her mother's desk. It was here that her mother worked her own kind of magic to promote their farm on the Internet. Elizabeth always knew when she was on the phone with city chefs because a little downstate accent crept into her voice. It was then that it was easy for Elizabeth to picture her mother as an important Manhattan advertising executive. Her speech was fast and quick and clever and she would twist up her hair into a bun and hold it there with a pen from the desk. She would bounce her crossed leg and Elizabeth could almost see an expensive high-heeled shoe instead of the dirty bare foot at the end of it.

Against the far wall sat an enormous rolltop desk that was full of nooks and drawers and secret compartments. This was her father's desk and when he was not working at it, the top was rolled down and locked. Elizabeth longed to go through all the drawers. It seemed to be a place that would hold secrets and treasures.

But there were treasures of sorts all around the office: mementos left behind by her father's family. She knew that the tin tractor on the shelf had been her grandfather's. The locked-up gun case had been built by her great grandfather from the wood of a cherry tree that used to be in the front yard. The stump of that cherry tree had become a tiered planter for a display of perennial flowers and had been one of the first places Elizabeth had been entrusted with the care of growing things. The quilt draped over the back of the couch was made by a great, great aunt named Mary Elizabeth Welles. Most exciting of all, to Elizabeth anyway, was the glass-fronted sideboard.

The sideboard was made to hold dishes and platters. But this sideboard held all kinds of Native American relics. There was a whole shelf of flint arrowheads in various shapes and sizes. A quiver made of deerskin lay on the lowest shelf. On the top shelf sat three pairs of beaded moccasins. The smallest were about the size of Elizabeth's hand. She loved to think about a little Indian child playing in the fields and creeks and maybe even climbing the trees of her valley, wearing those very moccasins.

Her father sat in his old wooden swivel chair and turned it to face Elizabeth. He leaned back and looked out the window to the right. There was the smallest sliver of gold and red still visible on the horizon, but the dark of night had firmly taken hold of the farm. He rocked gently and Elizabeth waited. Her father was also the kind of person who could not be rushed into speaking. She could hear the loud tick of the wall clock that had been made by her Great Uncle Mathias. The clock began to strike nine o'clock. When the echo of the ninth chime had almost diminished, her father rocked forward, slapped his hands to his knees, and smiled at Elizabeth. It was the thin, pretend smile.

"I have something for you!" he announced, his voice overly loud. He pulled his keys from his pocket and swiveled around to the rolltop desk. He unlocked it with a small, silver key and rolled back the slatted lid. He began to pull out small drawers and poke into the cubbies. "Ah," he sighed, and from a low, long shelf drew an item Elizabeth couldn't quite see.

When he swiveled back around, she could see that it was a knife in a sheath about six inches long. The sheath was leather and plain. It had four thin straps dangling off the back. The handle of the knife looked like it was made of some kind of bone. He handed it to Elizabeth. She ran her thumb along the handle.

"Your great grandmother's grandfather made that knife. He was a full-blood Seneca Indian. His daughter married a farmer who came from Connecticut and their daughter was your great grandmother. She was my Grandma Elizabeth and she was the smartest person I ever knew, at least until I met your mother!" Elizabeth looked up to see that her father was looking back out the window into the dark as he spoke.

"Grandma Elizabeth knew about every tree and every plant that grew in this valley. Whenever anyone was sick, Grandma Elizabeth had a tea or a tonic that helped. Sometimes she would simply tell them to sleep or laugh more. She would stand on the back porch every evening and scan the sky and announce to all of us what the weather would be like the next day and, I swear, she was never wrong.

"I asked her once, when I was about eight, how she always knew. She said the trees told her and," he paused to wink at Elizabeth, "she even told me about you!"

Elizabeth felt her eyes widen. Was this just a coincidence, or did her father somehow know about the bizarre events of the past two days? "What do you mean?" she asked.

Her father turned from the window and looked at her. He smiled and said, "You look a lot like her, and you definitely inherited her green thumb! Grandma Elizabeth told me that one day I would have a daughter and it was her wish that she be given her name. She also gave me that knife. I strapped it to my ankle every morning until I was about fourteen. It made me feel like an Indian and anytime I wasn't at school or doing chores, I was in the woods perfecting my tracking skills. I tracked a black bear once. I followed his trail to a patch of raspberries only to discover the bear still there!" Her father started to laugh at the memory.

"He rose up on his hind legs and fixed his beady black eyes on me. I grabbed the knife and stood my ground. I was shaking, but determined not to run. The bear, of course, dropped down and lumbered away. It was probably more annoyed than anything else at being disturbed in its berry picking. But I felt brave with that knife in my hand.

"I guess that is why I am giving it to you now. I need

you to be brave. I want you understand something Grandma Elizabeth told me. She said that it is important to know where we come from. She told me that the bones of my ancestors were in the soil of this land and that it is important to love it and respect it the way we love and respect each other. I believe that. I've done my best to honor my Grandma Elizabeth by honoring this land."

Her father furrowed his brow and his jaw tensed. He leaned forward in his chair and looked Elizabeth square in the eye. "Folks up and down the valley are selling their farms to Harmony Farms Incorporated. They are planning on making our valley into a series of feed lots to mass produce pigs and pork." Her father curled his lip and wrinkled his nose in disgust.

Elizabeth always thought the smell from the Danner farm was less than wonderful, but was puzzled by the feeling coming from her father's voice and expressions. "Don't the Danner's raise pigs?"

Her father's reply came out fast and held a hint of anger in it. "What Harmony Farms does is called factory farming and it's horrible for the animals, the people, the water, the air and especially the soil. Farming has become a business of 'get big or get out.' It doesn't seem to matter to some that factory farms ruin everything a farmer holds dear."

Elizabeth asked, "Why are they coming here? Why can't they go somewhere else?" Her father leaned back in his chair and covered his face with his hands.

"It seems we have the 'ideal' conditions: plenty of water, close proximity to a rail line and lots of corn growers to supply feed."

Elizabeth spoke again. "If it is so bad, why would people sell their farms to them?"

Her father sat back up. "Well kiddo, some folks think that money is the most important thing. They feel the more money they have, the happier they will be. Harmony Farms is paying a ton of money to buy these farms up. Farming is a tough life and I'm sure many people are thinking this is a way out that provides security."

Elizabeth stopped breathing, willing her next question to not even come to the front of her mind. It did. Elizabeth's voice trembled when she asked her next question. "Are you going to sell our farm?"

"No!" His voice was fierce. He jumped up and sent the chair rolling backwards into the desk. "I'm not selling to Harmony Farms, that's for damn sure!" He turned, and almost looked surprised that Elizabeth was sitting there. His voice softened. "No. I will do everything I can to stay here and to keep this land safe. My ancestors' blood is in the soil and I think, well, I think the soil is in our blood too, kiddo."

Elizabeth looked down at the knife in her lap. *The soil in our blood;* she hadn't thought of it before. She thought about everything Gaia had said that day. She thought about the fact that the vegetables they grew were the vegetables they ate. She thought about her great grandmother Elizabeth picking peas out of the same soil. She looked at the knife and wondered what she was going to do. What would any of them do?

Her mother leaned around the corner. "Elizabeth?" Elizabeth was startled from her thoughts. "I just got off the phone with Rachel's mother. They have invited us over for breakfast tomorrow. I said yes. After all, they're leaving in three days. I think we should go so you can say your goodbyes."

The thought of saying goodbye to Rachel amplified everything her father had said. Elizabeth jumped to her feet, the knife clutched in her right hand. "Say goodbye? Rachel can't go!" Her heart felt high and fluttery and weird. "And I won't go! I won't go! If they make you sell our farm, the factory pigs are just going to have to find room for me, because I won't go!" She ran past her mother, up the stairs, into her room and slammed the door. She stood on the other side of the door, breathing hard and clutching the knife.

She heard a familiar snuffling on the other side of the door. She opened it just enough to let Maizey in and then clicked it shut again. She knelt down on the floor and buried her face into Maizey's great fuzzy side. Her emotions waved back and forth between scared and mad. *Factory farms! What a horrible thought! Why would people want to do such a thing? I won't let them ruin Three Oaks and I won't go!* She sat back on her heels and looked into Maizey's big brown eyes. The dog was panting slightly, so she looked like she was smiling. *You wouldn't be smiling if you knew what was going on!*

"Listen up, Maizey. We're going to do something. We're going to talk to Gaia and we are going to do something. I won't let them ruin our farm. I won't." Maizey thumped her tail and continued to smile, as if in agreement.

16
Sneaking Out

Elizabeth knew her mother would come up to check on her and say good night. She would probably want to talk. Any other time, Elizabeth would welcome the chance to lie in the dark with the comfort of her mother's voice and the dip in the foot of the mattress where she sat. Her mother was the kind of person that wanted to be sure people talked through problems. As far as Elizabeth was concerned, there was no problem. She was going to save their farm, plain and simple.

She changed into her pajamas, brushed her teeth, climbed into bed and waited. After about twenty minutes, there was a soft knock on the door. Elizabeth was silent. There was a second knock and her mother called her name softly. Elizabeth closed her eyes and deepened her breath in anticipation of her mother's next move. Sure enough, the door opened a sliver. There was a long pause in which Elizabeth let her lower jaw fall slack and made sure to count to three each time she inhaled and exhaled. Her mother must have been satisfied, because the door closed with a slow and almost silent click and her sock feet could be heard padding down the stairs. *She'll still feel me out at breakfast.* When Elizabeth started that thought she felt annoyed, but by the end of the thought she was smiling inward to herself. Her mother was great. It was one more reason Elizabeth knew she had to learn as much as she could, as quickly as she could, from Gaia. She had to come up with a plan.

She lay in the dark listening to Maizey snort and twitch while chasing dream bunnies. She fought off waves of sleep by sitting up straight and reciting the Gettysburg Address to herself.

Fourscore and seven years ago our fathers brought forth on this continent a new nation, conceived in liberty and dedicated to the proposition that all men are created equal.

Now we are engaged in a great civil war, testing whether that nation or any nation so conceived and so dedicated can long endure. We are met on a great battlefield of that war. We have come to dedicate a portion of it as a final resting place for those who died here that the nation might live. This we may, in all propriety do. But in a larger sense, we cannot dedicate, we cannot consecrate, we cannot hallow this ground. The brave men, living and dead who struggled here have hallowed it far above our poor power to add or detract. The world will little note nor long remember what we say here, but it can never forget what they did here.

It is rather for us the living, we here be dedicated to the great task remaining before us--that from these honored dead we take increased devotion to that cause for which they here gave the last full measure of devotion--that we here

> highly resolve that these dead shall not have died in vain, that this nation shall have a new birth of freedom, and that government of the people, by the people, for the people shall not perish from the earth.

It was good to know something from fourth grade had stuck! She was just convincing herself that a long blink would do her eyes some good and that really, really she wouldn't fall asleep, when she heard the 11 o'clock news come on. She knew that her parents would be occupied for the next half hour. She climbed out of her bed as quietly as she could. She pulled off her pajamas and stuffed them under her pillow. She retrieved her dirty shorts and tee-shirt out of the hamper and slipped them on. Then she went to the window and pulled the screen out. She felt nervous and that made her turn back. She turned back to fetch the knife. With the old hard leather in her fist, she did feel braver.

Maizey picked up her large shaggy head and looked at Elizabeth with questions in her brown eyes. "Shhhhh, Maizey, I'll be gone a while. Be quiet until I get back." She went over the sill and onto the back porch's roof. She turned and looked back into the dark bedroom until Maizey dropped her head to her paws with a sigh. Elizabeth quietly sidestepped where the roof met the house. The small pebbles of the shingles hurt her feet and she felt stupid for not thinking to at least put on flip-flops. How was she going to save the farm when she couldn't even remember something as basic as shoes?

Off the end of the porch was one of the branches from the oak tree in the backyard. It looked like it was hugging the house. Elizabeth reached out her foot. She could get her bare foot firmly on the branch, but it was going to take a quick weight shift to step over that far. Elizabeth looked to see what she could grab onto if she pushed too hard. There was a small whip of a branch standing upright to her left. She took a deep breath and pushed off her back leg.

She thought she was safely off the roof and on the strong arm of The Chaplain. She was about to smile at this small accomplishment when a flash of dark, frantic, flickering motion caused her to flinch, stiffen and send her center of gravity over the big limb. Her jerk of panic was faster than her rational mind that knew that it was just a brown bat out eating bugs.

She found herself looking down at the ground on the other side. Her left hand shot out and grabbed the small upright branch. All her muscles tensed and her stomach lurched when it bent like a reed in the wind. *NO!* Elizabeth thought, expecting to feel the hard thud of the ground. But to her amazement, the little whip of a branch stiffened up and pulled her back to vertical on to the big limb.

Elizabeth panted, adrenaline coursing through her veins. She steadied herself and was just starting to wonder why, when she looked down at her feet, all ten toes curled tightly around the limb. She smiled. *Thank you,* she thought down through her feet and into the tree. The limb gave three small bounces and all the leaves on that limb danced and twirled on their stems. Elizabeth stood still, her heart bursting with the realization that she just had a conversation with her beloved oak tree. She shuffled down the length of the tree branch, grateful that she wasn't wearing flip-flops. When she reached the main trunk, she turned and sat straddled on the branch, her back against the trunk. She felt the pattern of the bark through her tee-shirt, pressing into her back. Yes, she was going to do everything in her power to save the farm. The only question in her mind now, was how much power did she have?

She closed her eyes and thought, *Gaia, Gaia, Gaia.*

17
Traveling

Elizabeth wasn't sure how long she sat that way, silently thinking Gaia's name and wondering just what it was she was going to ask Gaia to do. Maybe Gaia was in China talking to some other girl right now. Maybe this wasn't the way to call Gaia at all. Maybe there was no Gaia and she had just hit her head really hard at some point and had been imagining all this. That last thought began to creep up more and more as Elizabeth got colder and colder in the damp night air.

She sat and went over all the events of the past few days: meeting Gaia in the sheep pasture, her accidental tree trip to school, the meeting in the creek, the fairy ring, and the thrill of the dancing aspens.

That's it! Gaia had said she made that place just for her and just for today. Elizabeth decided to try the reverse of what she had done just a few hours ago. She thought of the aspen trees in their neat ring, out in the woods. She pictured the rock in the center of the circle and the soft smell of violets. She let the song of the aspens fill her imagination. She thought, *Please send me to the fairy ring*. She instantly felt the bark at her back push against her more intensely, and then all went dark. Deep wood smells filled her nostrils and her body again felt bent and twisted and flung about. This time, although it was still quite uncomfortable, Elizabeth didn't feel afraid. She was hoping this was what would happen.

She felt an upward rushing sensation and found herself sitting high in thin branches waving side to side. She knew by the spinning leaves around her that this was a trembling aspen. The tree seemed to be applauding her arrival. *Good job! Good job!*

She did it! She moved herself! She was elated until she realized there was no safe way to climb down. The aspen had a thin trunk and even smaller branches. She clung to one of the aspen's high fragile branches, wondering what she had gotten herself into.

Then she remembered her dance with the trees earlier that day. She took a deep breath and thought, *Please lower me to the ground.* The aspen did an impossibly deep bow and deposited her into the circle.

Now what? Fog had crept up out of the nearby creek and was snaking across the ground. It looked like every scary movie that Elizabeth had ever seen. She realized that she still had the knife in her hand, so she gripped it tighter. She thought a real Indian would never be afraid of a fairy ring in the dark. So she stood a little taller and marched purposefully out to the center of the ring. There! Brave! Her father would be proud of her.

She climbed up on the rock and lay on her back. Above her, small but heavy clouds moved quickly across the sky, giving the illusion that stars were being turned on and off. She wondered if Gaia had spoken to any of these stars. She would have to remember to ask. Where was Gaia? How could she call out to her? Did Gaia know about the big pig farm coming? Was that why she was in a hurry? The questions blinked on and off like the stars.

Elizabeth wasn't sure when she fell asleep, but waking up to a stiff back pressed against a cold rock is memorable. She pushed herself upright and looked around. It was deep night. She shivered and wished Maizey were with her. It was so quiet and still that Elizabeth wondered if time itself was standing still. A large barred owl silently passed across the open circle to belie that thought. Elizabeth shuddered. The owl's silent appearance was like the way Gaia had slipped into her life, unannounced. And, like a mouse's surprise at the silent attack from the owl, Elizabeth felt ambushed by the events around her. Her farm was threatened, her parents were acting weird, and her best friend was moving.

Maybe it was because she had finally gotten a bit of sleep, or it could have been the fresh night air, but an idea came to her with an almost audible "POP." She pushed off the rock and ran across the circle to one of the aspens. She wrapped her arms around the tree and squeezed her eyes closed and began to imagine another familiar tree: the one supporting Rachel's tree house.

When she found herself in the maple at the end of Rachel's driveway, she wanted to shout with triumph. Two times she had traveled all by herself. Gaia wasn't there. She felt a new sense of strength rising in her like sap rising in the trees she loved.

She and Rachel had spent long hours in the tree house that was now just a few branches below. The route down was familiar, so she quickly dropped to the ground. She made her way up the gravel drive, again wishing for flip-flops. The Winters' house was dark and Elizabeth was thankful they had no dog. She tried to move as quietly as the barred owl around the side of the house. The last ground floor window was Rachel's and it was wide open.

Elizabeth put her mouth close to the screen and hissed, "Rachel!" She heard a snort and a murmur. "Rachel!" she hissed again. She heard the creak of bedsprings and then silence. "Rachel! It's me, Elizabeth!" She heard a more pronounced bedspring squeak as Rachel left her bed. Her face appeared at the screen, eyes red rimmed and squinting.

"What are you doing? How did you get here? It's two in the morning!" Rachel said, her voice low and gravelly with sleep.

Elizabeth grinned. "Rachel, I know you're mad at me, but I've got to tell you what's been going on!"

"Packing! That's what's been going on! I'm moving and you don't even care." Rachel looked a little mad, but mostly sad. She rubbed her fists against her eyes and yawned wide.

"No! Listen, I care a lot! You're my best friend! Why wouldn't I care?"

Rachel pouted and looked at the windowsill. "I

thought you were mad at me because you weren't going to get to go to Disney World." Elizabeth couldn't help herself. She started to laugh.

Rachel stood up. Elizabeth could only see her nightgown, but heard her say, "What's so funny?"

"Open the screen and let me in. The mosquitoes are having me for hors d'oeuvres and I don't want to be the main course while I explain."

Rachel knelt back down and said, "Listen, I don't want to get in trouble and I bet you would catch all kinds of heck if your folks knew you were here at two in the morning. Aren't you coming for breakfast? Can't you tell me then?"

"Sure, but I want you to see something." She hadn't been sure if she should share, but Rachel had been her best friend since they were five years old. Elizabeth took about ten steps back to an old twisted plum tree. She pressed her back against it and turned her palms back until she felt its woody trunk. In her mind's eye she saw the familiar spread of branches that were the arms of The Chaplain. *Please, send me home.* As she felt the plum tree's trunk begin to press harder against her back, she began to giggle. Rachel's face was comprised of three big circles: two bulging eyes and a wide-open mouth.

The trip home was fast and not nearly as uncomfortable, now that she knew what was happening. Once safely in her own oak tree, Elizabeth quickly made her way back to the porch roof and to her own window. As she pulled herself over the sill, Maizey leapt up and uttered a loud, "WOOF." "Shhhhhh, it's me!" Maizey wagged and yawned and set about intensely sniffing Elizabeth's feet. Elizabeth heard the loud click of the light switch in the hallway. The crack under the door lit up!

She dove into bed, clothes and all and squeezed her eyes closed. Behind her eyelids she saw the light increase as her door was cracked open. Knowing that she couldn't fake a deep sleep, which would be weird considering Maizey just let out a woof to wake the dead, she did a toss and a turn and fluttered her eyelids sleepily, "Huh? Wha?" She hoped she looked groggy.

"Go back to sleep. Maizey must be chasing dream

bunnies again." Her father called the great dog and Elizabeth fell back to her pillow and began to breathe deeply. He never noticed her screen was out.

18
Breakfast at Rachel's

Elizabeth was deep in a black hole. There was nothing to look at, nothing to think about, and that felt really wonderful. A voice was coming from a far distant place. It was an insistent voice. She wanted to ignore it. The voice knew her name. It was her mother's voice and that started to remind her of who she was. It took Elizabeth a long time to realize that her mother was actually shaking her and scolding her too.

"What have I told you about sleeping in dirty clothes? My God! Look at these mosquito bites! No wonder you're bit up, your screen is out. Didn't you notice your screen was out? Maizey must have knocked it out. Elizabeth, we have to leave in twenty minutes. It's time to quit stalling and get up!"

Elizabeth rolled out of bed and immediately began to scratch her arm, her knee, her neck and thirty-seven other places the mosquitoes had played Red Cross Blood Drive on her last night. As she brushed her teeth, she realized how ironic it was that her mistake of leaving the screen out had provided a nice explanation as to why she was covered with bites. *Mental note: bug spray.*

She was yawning on the outside, but inside, she was excited. She was going to tell Rachel all about her adventures. Maybe she could have Gaia teach Rachel some things too! Maybe they could travel the world together and it wouldn't matter that Rachel was moving! This last thought added a bounce to Elizabeth's feet as she went down the stairs.

When they stepped off the front porch, her mother looked up at the sky. Fog still hugged the ground, lit from behind by weak sunlight. It was as if the day couldn't decide what its mood was going to be. "What do you think, Elizabeth? Should we ride our bikes over, or do you think we will get rained on?

Elizabeth looked at the reddish glow in the East. *Red at night, sailors delight. Red in the morning, sailors take warning.* That little poem was a very useful way to make a guess at the weather. She waved at the gnats in front of her eyes; the detested little black bugs were intent on biting, and that confirmed the sky's story. "It's going to rain. Let's drive."

Her mother kept quiet for the first three minutes in the car, but then she asked, "What do you think about Rachel moving?"

"I think it stinks." There, that was a simple answer that would probably preclude additional questions. But it didn't.

"Did you know her father is going to work at the Harmony Farms Headquarters?"

"No." She wanted to ask why, but didn't really want to know the answer. This bit of news meant that Mr. Winters was going to be getting a paycheck from the enemy. That was how Elizabeth was beginning to view Harmony Farms. Did that make Mr. Winters the enemy too? What about Rachel? How could her best friend so suddenly be part of something that was turning her life upside down?

Her mother didn't say anything else until they turned into the Winters' driveway. "Listen, honey. I am going to ask that you try to be the bigger person today. Mrs. Winters told me Rachel isn't dealing well with all this. She is angry. She is probably going to be mean to the people she trusts the most. That includes you, OK? Cut her a little slack. You guys are best friends and best friends have a way of working through things."

Elizabeth simply nodded and jumped out of the car. Rachel was waiting on the porch. The wicker patio furniture was set around a table topped with bagels and tea, orange juice and raspberries. Mrs. Winters had that overly cheerful voice of an adult who wants everyone to pretend everything is OK. "Good morning! What a beautiful day we're going to have, don't you think?"

Elizabeth thought it was a ridiculous question, given that the sky was growing heavier by the minute. Besides, if anyone took the time to tilt their nose up and smell, the distant tang of thunder was on the air.

"Sit! Sit! Tea? Yes, I think we are going to be blessed with a perfect summer day as soon as the last of this fog burns off." Mrs. Winter's cheerfulness hung in the air as heavy as the fog.

Rachel sat looking at Elizabeth, but not saying anything. It made Elizabeth feel strange. They usually "chatted like jays." That is what her mother often said, comparing them to blue jays. It was strange to be sitting with Rachel and not see her wide, toothy grin. It was strange not to have Rachel grabbing her arms and exclaiming, "Guess what?"

Elizabeth didn't want to be the first one to speak, so she poured some orange juice into a glass and sat back to sip. She couldn't wait to tell Rachel about the otter and the trees and the way she knocked Dell Danner on his butt. She could feel a grin sneaking up to her mouth and pressed her lips together to stop it. If Elizabeth could have seen herself, she would have seen a striking similarity to her father, dimples deepening in anticipation of the laugh.

Rachel stood up and turned to her mother. "Can we take our food out to the tree fort?" Elizabeth felt some hope in her heart. *Rachel isn't mad! We will sit in the fort and I will tell her what has been going on.* Elizabeth hurried to gather up her food, tucking it into a bag that Rachel's mother brought out.

A few minutes later they were climbing up the ladder, shooing gnats from their eyes and setting out their breakfast. Elizabeth sat down cross-legged on the floor and grinned at Rachel. Rachel, on the other hand, sat down cross-legged on the floor and scowled at Elizabeth. Elizabeth's smile faded away as she realized this wasn't going to be a fun conversation about talking otters and tree transportation.

"I thought you were my best friend!" Rachel said.

Her voice was dense with accusation. The words hung between them like overripe fruit.

Elizabeth felt like she had been kicked. "I am! Rachel, you never gave me a chance to talk to you and then everything has been so weird these past few days. I wanted to tell you everything last night, but you wouldn't let me in!"

Rachel's eyes went wide and her mouth opened. Elizabeth almost started laughing because it was almost the exact same face she had seen in the window the night before.

"I dreamed you were at my window," Rachel said, her voice small.

"I was!" Elizabeth jumped up and started pacing around the tree house. "That's what I have been trying to tell you! I met this otter. Only she isn't really an otter at all, but she is like the whole world. But not really the world, more like the earth all packaged up in this otter body. It's hard to explain. Have you ever thought about your little toe?" Rachel too, was on her feet and her face was a mix of hurt and confusion.

"My toe? What are you talking about? I'M MOV-

ING! Don't you care at all?" Elizabeth ran over and hugged her best friend. Her body was stiff.

"I care. I care so much. I don't want you to go, but Rachel, I can move through trees!" She held Rachel out at arm's length and searched her eyes. Rachel's eyes widened for a moment, but then they seemed to cool and retreat.

"I don't believe you," Rachel said. "You're being selfish. You get to stay here. *I'm* the one who has to go live in Orlando and go to a new school and not be able to swim in the creek anymore. *I'm* the one who has to go where there aren't any hills and nothing but skinny, stupid palm trees. I think you're selfish and I don't believe you!"

Elizabeth felt as sad and dark as the deepening sky outside. She scratched one of the many red bites on her arm and tensed her jaw. How could she prove to Rachel that she cared? How could she make her see that this was not pretend, but real? She closed her eyes and took a deep breath. As she exhaled it was as if her ears got bigger and she could hear the jangling of the plum tree, whispering, *"Show her, show her."*

She stepped to the back of the tree fort where the floor met the trunk of the tree. She leaned back against the trunk, never letting her eyes leave Rachel's angry stare. She said, "See you up at the house." She closed her eyes and saw the plum tree in the Winters' side yard. She saw it and heard it and asked with respect to be there. *Please.* Was it her imagination, or was the whole process of being sucked into the bark getting less painful?

Elizabeth stepped forward into the Winters' yard. She could hear her mother and Mrs. Winters laughing on the screened porch. How could grown-ups laugh when something so horrible was happening?

She moved to the corner of the house and looked down the driveway. She could see Rachel dropping off the last step of the ladder and turning to jog up the drive. When Rachel was almost to the house, Elizabeth stepped out. Rachel pulled up short and stood gaping at Elizabeth. Elizabeth held out her arms and sang out, "Ta-Da!"

Rachel closed her eyes and shook her head. There was a long moment. It seemed like the air was now pressing in on all sides. A sudden gust of wind seemed to send the temperature up a few degrees. Sweat sprang out on Elizabeth's lip. She licked it away and waited for Rachel to say something. It felt like a moment of truth.

Rachel opened her eyes and yelled, "I hate you! You're no friend! You're playing tricks on me! Go home!" She turned and ran past the stunned grown-ups and into the house. A moment later, the muffled bang of a slammed door could be heard from the back of the house.

Elizabeth looked through the screen at her mother and Mrs. Winters. It was bad enough that Rachel had said such a thing, but the fact that it was said in front of their mothers made the orange juice in her stomach turn sour. Between the increasing heat and humidity and the tension of the moment, Elizabeth wondered if the orange juice might make a sudden reappearance.

Her mother set down her coffee and stood up. "Well Joyce, we should be going. I know you have a lot of work to do." Mrs. Winters followed her mother out the door and came down to where Elizabeth stood. She then knelt down and gave her a hug.

"Please don't be mad at Rachel," she whispered in Elizabeth's ear. "She is mad at the whole world right now. I'll make sure to get the phone and computer hooked up as fast as I can so you girls can e-mail and chat, OK?" She sat back on her heels and smiled at Elizabeth.

It was then that it really hit her. Rachel was really going. And her mom would be gone too. And Elizabeth would never be in their house again. She would never eat lunch at their kitchen table again. She wouldn't hear silly knock-knock jokes from Rachel's dad! The truth hit her so hard she couldn't breathe.

She could feel hot tears stinging her eyes and her nose filled up with snot. "Goodbye Mrs. Winters! Thanks for everything." And with that she turned and ran to the car. She flung herself into the backseat and cried. The sky opened up and cried with her.

19
Teatime

The nice thing about a rainy day is it allows you to really wallow in your bad mood. The rain streaming down the windows was the perfect backdrop for Elizabeth's sadness. She lay on the sofa and stared through the office doorway at the breakfront. Her mother had stopped in once to ask if Elizabeth was hungry, once to ask if she wanted to watch television (something Elizabeth couldn't remember her ever actually encouraging!), and once more to ask if she needed anything. Elizabeth said, "No, I just wanna lay here." Maizey, because she was such a good dog, lay on the floor right next to her and acted just as blue.

She let her arm hang off the couch and her fingers twined through Maizey's hair. Her thoughts swung like a pendulum back and forth from Rachel to Gaia, from her friend to her farm. She wanted to fix things with Rachel, but in her belly was an instinct to take care of herself and her family. The soil was in her blood and she was brave.

She could hear her mother in the office typing furiously on the computer keyboard, click clickity click. Her mother often used rainy days to update the Three Oaks' website and write her customer newsletter. The clickity, click click along with the staccato of the rain was hypnotic. Elizabeth scratched her bug bites and then slid off into the sleep she had missed the night before.

It was hours later (how long is hard to tell on a rainy day) when she began to float up towards wakefulness and heard a soft musical voice. Gaia! She rolled off the couch and ran from window to window, looking out through the rain, looking for the galumphing otter shape. Maizey ran with her, looking for the cause of such excitement. They ended up on the back porch, looking out across the yard toward the big barn. There was nothing to be seen but rain and low clouds.

She continued to scan through the grayness of the day until she heard her stomach growl. Maizey heard it too and cocked her head. Elizabeth laughed at the dog's quizzical face. "Listen Maizey, I never actually ate breakfast! Let's go see what's in the kitchen."

After an egg salad sandwich and a large, cold glass of milk, Elizabeth felt alert and revived and ready to fight the world. She cleared her dishes and turned to Maizey. "Are you going to help me save the farm?" Maizey gave an affirmative, "WOOF" and wagged her tail against the table leg. Elizabeth could still hear the clickity click of the computer keyboard so she went to the office doorway.

"Mom?"

"Mmmm, Hmmmm?" Clickity, click. Her mother didn't look up.

"Can I go down to the creek?"

"No. It's raining." The keyboard stopped clicking and her mother swiveled around in her chair. She pulled off her glasses and leveled a good long mom stare at Elizabeth. "No. You haven't been exactly well and it's raining. I would prefer that we don't start off the summer with you getting sick!

"As a matter of fact," she stood, crossed the room and headed to the kitchen. "I think we are both a little stressed." She looked over her shoulder at Elizabeth, stuck up her nose and lowered her eyelids, "Teatime, Dahling?"

Elizabeth loved her mother's 'snobby voice.' She replied, "Oh yes, Dahling! Tea would be lovely!" Teatime was a favorite for Elizabeth.

Her mother would spread a lacy tablecloth and set the table with delicate china plates, tea cups, and saucers. The china was off-white and rimmed with violets and buttercups. When Elizabeth settled into her chair, she was surprised to realize that the design on the cups and saucers was almost identical to the flowers of the fairy ring Gaia had taken her to.

Her mother soon brought over the teapot filled with steaming water.

"Earl Grey?"

Elizabeth wrinkled her nose and shook her head. Earl Grey was a black tea and always tasted harsh to Elizabeth.

"May I have raspberry, please?" Elizabeth said in what she hoped sounded like a good snobby voice.

"Why of course! We have a lovely dried raspberry leaf, picked by a beautiful maiden in an enchanted land."

Elizabeth smiled. Her mother meant her. She had picked the raspberry leaves last summer and had helped dry them and package them into little packets. Her mother opened a packet now and put the dried leaves into a metal ball that went into the teapot. As the hot water began to draw out the flavor from the leaves, her mother brought a tray of shortbread cookies to the table and then sat down.

After she had poured them each a cup, she raised her cup delicately and said, in the snobby voice, "Oh Dahling, did you hear the latest news?"

"No Dahling, do tell."

"It seems that The Winters have bought a new estate in Florida! You know Florida is just all the rage." Her mother's eyes peered over the edge of her teacup.

Elizabeth dunked her cookie into her tea and thought a minute. Even when playing teatime, Elizabeth wasn't one to be quick to speak. "Well, I hear that Florida is perfectly dreadful. It is hot and has alligators and very large bugs. Civilized people summer here, upstate, dahling."

Her mother set her cup down with a sharp clank. "Well, Dahling. I think it is incumbent upon us civilized people to write to the Winters and let them know how much they are missed in Upstate New York society. I know! I will ring the stationers and order Young Miss Elizabeth some fine linen stationery so that she may learn the art of letter writing."

"Mom!" Elizabeth giggled, falling out of teatime mode. "We have e-mail and instant message!"

Her mother smiled and finished her tea. As she began to clear the china she said, "Elizabeth, there is nothing in the world like receiving a letter, especially if the sender writes from her heart. You'll understand someday."

"Can I at least go chat with her now? I want to apologize and say goodbye."

"Well, we haven't really set up summer rules for computer use, but seeing as it's raining buckets outside, go ahead. One hour, tops, and be sure to log me off first and shut everything down when you're done."

Elizabeth tore out of the kitchen like her feet were on fire. She was not fired up to e-mail Rachel. She figured Rachel's computer was probably boxed up by now, but, while she had been sipping her tea, she realized she could use the computer to help save her farm.

In order to win a war, one must know her enemy. She was going to use the Internet to find out all she could about Harmony Farms. She wanted to know about these factory farms. She wasn't sure how that would help, but it was better than knowing nothing at all. Besides, it gave her something to do on this sad, wet day. It always feels good to take action.

She found that she wasn't the only one in her family with that thought. When she sat down at the computer, she quickly found that her mother had been viewing the Harmony Farms website. Their logo was a cheery red barn and silo. Above the barn was a bright, shiny sun with the words Harmony Farms arched over it. She began to read through their site.

Boy, they made it all sound so great. Harmony Farms was feeding a hungry world and doing it cheaply. She saw a picture of their headquarters in Orlando, Florida and tried to picture Rachel's dad in one of the windows. It made her feel weird. But not as weird as what she saw next.

Elizabeth went to the other websites her mother had been viewing. Her tea and cookie began to feel like lead in her belly. These sites showed her what factory farming really was. Such farms were called CAFOs, Concentrated Animal Feeding Organizations. The pictures she saw were disgusting. Pigs were crammed so close together they bit each other's tails off! Chickens had their beaks burned dull. Cows were pumped full of antibiotics and things called growth hormones and then killed by shooting a bolt into their brains. And it got worse.

The so-called farms were row after row of metal sheds. The thousands of animals inside had to poop, just like all animals do, but there were so many of them pooping and peeing that the air for miles around had toxic chemicals in it. The poop ran off into streams and rivers and ruined them. People living near these places had to move because they had asthma attacks and there were giant swarms of flies. They couldn't drink their well water anymore. There were places where you couldn't even put your toe in the stream because the water was like poison! She looked at page after page of pictures and felt her spine growing tight and cold.

Did people really keep animals like this? Did they really think that this was good, healthy food? She went back to the Harmony Farms site and stared at the logo. It was like a big lie. The happy red barn was something you could see here in Avon, but nothing at all like the rows of sheds that had miserable animals inside them.

Elizabeth began to shut down the computer. She hoped that Gaia had more tricks up her sleeve than just the wonder of tree travel! *Gaia, where are you? We've got to hurry!*

20
Where is Gaia?

For the next few weeks nothing new happened. It didn't seem like summer. It rained a lot and the days were cool. It seemed like the sky was crowding down close to their heads all the time and the ground beneath their feet was sodden and spongy.

The Fourth of July fireworks were rained out. The Angiers and the Jeffries celebrated by having a sad, damp picnic under the arms of The Chaplain. The grown-ups mostly talked low to each other about farming and growth and change. Will joked and played with Maizey, but Elizabeth mostly sat and watched and sighed along with the leaves of The Chaplain.

Elizabeth couldn't work in the garden because the ground was too wet. She didn't have to water the trees, and it was too cold to go swimming in the creek. Even feeding the sheep was a little irritating. The smell of wet wool, a smell she loved in winter, made her all the more aware that this wasn't a usual summer. The month of July seemed like some kind of weird, depressing non-season.

One drippy Thursday afternoon, Will came over and played checkers with her. After Elizabeth beat him twice, he taught her how to play chess, but Elizabeth found it hard to concentrate. They were sitting on the back porch and she kept glancing over toward Sing Song Creek, hoping to see the brown, galumphing shape of Gaia. Didn't otters like the rain? *Where is she? Where is Gaia?* That recurring thought had become almost automatic in her mind, ringing out once every five minutes.

"Hey Lizzy! You can't move a rook that way."

"Huh? I thought the castle could go kitty-corner."

"That's the bishop that does that. And call it a rook. Only amateurs call it a castle!"

"In case you hadn't notice, Mr. Jeffries, I am an amateur! I don't like this game anyway. Checkers is more fun."

Will sat back in his chair and also looked off toward the creek. He laced his fingers and propped his hands behind his head.

"This weather stinks, doesn't it?" he said.

"You know what really stinks? Big Pig CAFOs! That's what stinks! They stink so bad no one can live around them!"

Will shook his head and smiled at her. "I should have known you would know what was going on. I think it stinks too. Want to hear the biggest stinker of them all?"

"What?" Elizabeth held her breath, not wanting any more bad news.

"My dad thinks I should get a job with Harmony Farms. Can you believe my dad thinks I should kill and carve up pigs for a living?" It was the kind of question that didn't require an answer. "Disassembling, they call it." Elizabeth could see the disgust on his face.

She couldn't imagine Will doing such a thing. Tall, skinny, laughing Will with his big brown eyes and quick smile disassembling pigs? She felt the coldness returning to her spine. Should she tell him about Gaia? Could he help her think of a plan? Maybe if he knew he could help find her.

"Aren't you going to college?" Elizabeth asked.

"I don't really have the grades, Lizzy. Besides, my folks don't have that kind of money. That is part of the reason they want me to work for Harmony Farms. My dad says I could work my way up to management someday and that I would have benefits and all this other stuff that is supposed to make me think that working for them is a good thing. He thinks dairy farming isn't the business it used to be and that I need to become part of the 'get big' method of livestock farming."

Elizabeth could tell by the tone in his voice that Will thought working for Harmony Farms was about the worst thing in the world.

Will sat forward again. "Enough about me and my big pig dilemma. What are you missing most this summer, Lizzy?"

"Rachel." Elizabeth didn't see any need to say anything else about that. Rachel hadn't sent her a new e-mail address or been on AIM or called, or anything.

"Besides Rachel."

"Sunshine. And sitting up in The Scout."

The platform in the oak high on the ridge had no roof and although Elizabeth longed to sit high up and look out over her beloved farm, she just wasn't into getting cold and wet.

"Ah! Makes sense. Well Lizard, I should get down to help your dad. I know the garden is a bit of a bust this year, but those rich suburbanites still want their ornamental trees!"

"OK, Buffalo Breath. You going to the Farmer's

Market on Saturday?

"Well sure! People want their milk and cheese! What all do you have to take down anyway?"

Elizabeth thought about the produce they had available. Everything was slow in coming. All the lettuces were small and limp. The tomatoes seemed determined not to grow until the sun came out. It was as if the garden itself had heard the Harmony Farms news and didn't want to grow until it knew what was going to happen.

She shrugged her shoulders. "We may just do a delivery and not even go to the market; maybe just some wool and wildflowers."

"Well," he stood, "You don't need my help with that girly stuff!"

Elizabeth stuck out her tongue at him. He gave her a wink and rubbed Maizey between the ears before heading out the back door.

Elizabeth began to clean up the chess pieces and checkers. She thought about poor Will. What would he be able to do now that Harmony Farms was going to take over all the farms in the area? She felt the warmth of the leather sheath and the solidness of the knife against her ankle and smiled a little. If she and Gaia had anything to do with it, Harmony Farms would have to go somewhere else!

Where was Gaia anyway? Elizabeth sat back down and closed her eyes. She began to pay attention to the pattern of rain on the roof and the syncopation of the raindrops rolling off the leaves of The Chaplain. She could hear the low rumble of Sing Song Creek. It no longer laughed and sparkled, but was thick and heavy and hurried.

She spent the next hour awash in the song of all the living things around her. The song was not at all like the high, happy one she had heard in the fairy ring. Like the leaden sky above, the music seemed to be slow and sad. The question of Gaia's whereabouts continued to surface, so where Elizabeth sensed an opening in the music, she inserted a call to Gaia in the song. *Gaia, please come.*

21
The Soil is in My Blood

Elizabeth woke to the sound of shouting. She bounded out of bed and down the stairs. Her father stood in the middle of the kitchen waving the newspaper and yelling, "They can't just bribe us like this! It doesn't make any of it right! I notice that it doesn't say when the next planning meeting is." Her father slapped the paper on the table and stormed out the back door.

Elizabeth looked at the headline.

HARMONY FARMS TO FUND MAJOR SCHOOL EXPANSION!

AVON CENTRAL TO BE STATE-OF-THE-ART FACILITY

She looked up at her mother. "What does this mean?" Her mother had a blank expression on her face and was chewing her lower lip.

"It means that anyone who doesn't want to cooperate with Harmony Farms will look like a real bad guy." And she didn't say anymore, just continued to chew her lower lip and stare at her coffee cup.

Elizabeth went back to her room, Maizey at her heels. She dressed quickly. *Yuk, long pants again.* It was absurd to be wearing long pants in the middle of summer, but it was just too cool for shorts. She finished by strapping the knife to her ankle. She pulled her pant leg down over it and gave it a pat. Her dad was right; it did make her feel braver. She went back to the kitchen. Her mother was now reading the paper. Elizabeth grabbed a peach from the bowl on the counter.

"I'm going outside," she announced. She waited for her mother to look up. Would she see the determination in Elizabeth? Elizabeth had made a decision. She could no longer wait for Gaia. Something had to be done now.

Her mother mumbled, "OK, but stay out of the creek; we had a lot of rain yesterday." She never looked up.

Elizabeth thought her mother's statement was silly. It had rained almost every day and it was still so cool and damp that Sing Song Creek held no attraction. It was muddy brown and full of debris.

She headed across the lawn. It was glistening with dewdrops and the rain-soaked soil gave a small squelch with each step. Maizey bounded past her and around the barn. She heard Maizey let out a string of happy barks. She jogged around the big barn and there, down by the creek in the long morning shadows of the willow trees, was the distinct curved figure of an otter.

Elizabeth breathed a sigh and waved. The otter rose up, waved back and then turned and dove into the underbrush beneath the willows. Where was Gaia going? Maizey ran down to the entrance of the path and Elizabeth followed. Standing in the cold of the shaded path, Elizabeth saw a small black pointed snout poking out of the water. "Follow me," Gaia called and her voice sounded like the music of morning dew-drops.

Gaia went off downstream and Maizey and Elizabeth had to jog to keep up. Elizabeth never knew that otters were so quick in the water! They had gone past the swimming hole before Gaia pulled her gleam-ing sleek form from the water. She shook and the spray sparkled in the ever-increasing sunlight.

The sun was actually coming out today! Feeling the warmth of the rising sun on her back along with seeing Gaia gave Elizabeth a sense of finally being able to exhale, as if she had been holding her breath for weeks.

Elizabeth planted her hands on her hips and said,

"Where have you been? I thought you were in this big hurry!" The otter laughed and it sounded like a thousand small streams rolling down a thousand mountainsides.

"Hello again, my dear. I had other business to attend to. There are dire things going on all around me! Please remember, it takes a tremendous amount of energy for me to put all my consciousness in this form, and only be here. I can't do it all the time! Now, as I had said before, we need to be quick."

"I know! Gaia, they are going to take our farm away and build some horrible pig factory thing! I've got to stop it, but I don't know what to do! I've been waiting and waiting for you to come back!"

"Let's skip the hysterics and get to work, shall we?" Gaia began to circle around Elizabeth while she spoke. "In time, you will have many powers, but for right now we need to focus on the things that can help you the most. I need you to practice with the trees."

"But Gaia, I've been practicing. Watch this!"

Without thinking, Elizabeth stepped to the nearest willow and wrapped her arms around it. She pictured her oak tree at the end of the driveway. *Please, I would like to go home.* She heard Maizey launch into a frenzy of barking and was all the way into the dark and twisting process before she realized her mistake! Next thing she knew, she was perched high above the Three Oaks sign at the end of her driveway.

Far off she could hear Maizey barking. *That was stupid!* She gripped the oak tighter and thought, *Please, I would like to go back to the willow.* She was actually getting familiar with the push of the bark and the twisting and turning and deep, dark woods smells.

To her surprise, she found herself in a familiar place, but the wrong place. She was in the crook in her reading tree by the bridge! *Grrrrr.* She jumped down and took off at a run down the path. Rounding the bend at the swimming hole, she was knocked completely off her feet. She crashed to the ground and didn't even have time to wonder what had happened before the flurry of dog kisses told her. Maizey must have been heading home on the path, looking for her!

Gaia pulled herself out of the creek and waddled over. She was shaking with laughter and it sounded like the toe bells of fairies. "Oh dear! That is what you get for showing off! I do not doubt your ability, or I never would have chosen you. You do need direction, though. There is more to trees than their names! Get up."

Elizabeth climbed up and began swiping mud off her knees and elbows. Maizey continued to lick her and look contrite. Gaia rose up on her hind legs and said, "I started you out with trees because you seem to love and understand them. You now have to understand the earth itself, the very soil you walk upon."

The soil that is in my blood! Elizabeth thought. She felt a little more confident; her Great Grandmother Elizabeth had said that her family's blood was in the soil and the soil was in their blood. She felt she was about to learn something of great importance. Gaia continued.

"I guess that the bright minds of your world have proper scientific names for everything I am about to say; if you want to know those things, you will have to learn that yourself. I do not expect you to know the name the third cell of your pinky toe has for blood, so please do not expect me to know what humans call the movement of mountains.

I hope that you know that right now you are floating. What feels so solid and dense beneath your infinitesimally small feet is fluid and moving and changing all the time. Mountains rise and fall, all the large landmasses move and slide and drift about. I change. I change, and it is this slow turnover of material that has, in part, allowed so much life to exist."

Elizabeth looked at the muddy packed earth beneath her feet. *Fluid?* Her mind conjured up the map in her classroom and the remarkable way that South America, if you could slide it across the Atlantic Ocean, would fit neatly into Africa. Elizabeth knew that continents moved, but she always felt that this was something that happened 'before' and wasn't actually happening now.

Gaia had resumed her circular lecture pacing. "Someday you and I will go very deep into my being. It would be a dangerous journey for you now, and I will not take you to my depths until it is necessary. You cannot go all the way. There is another who will dive into my heart, into the fire."

There was a pause and then Gaia continued. "So today we will keep it small and easy. We will do things that give you some confidence. I am going to remind you that you have done this before."

"I have?"

"In your schoolyard, you marshaled the soil to do your will. Do you remember?"

Elizabeth remembered the anger flowing through her feet and sending the dirt in a wave form to knock Dell onto his bully butt. "I remember. But Gaia, I didn't mean to do that."

"Precisely. You have talent and I have given you permissions, but you need to learn the finer points in order to have control. Being mad is never helpful. Now, let us try something easy. Take off your shoes; it will work better." Elizabeth stood in her bare feet and listened to what Gaia wanted her to try. She felt doubtful, but when she stopped to feel the knife tied against her lower leg, she set the doubt aside.

She took a deep breath and sent her idea down into her feet. She kept her eyes closed and had a vague sensation of movement. She opened her eyes in time to see a little ripple of dirt rush up behind Maizey and bump into her back paws. Maizey spun around, but seeing nothing of concern, resumed her position, nose into the breeze.

Elizabeth smiled. Gaia smiled, except otters don't really smile; it was more of a pleased posture. "Good!" Gaia sang out and it sounded like the twitter of a hundred goldfinches. "Go bigger this time, really push and send it into the creek." Elizabeth repeated the process. This time, she could feel the rumble of the movement and waited until she heard the splash and pitter pat of dirt falling into the stream before she opened her eyes.

She felt a lift in her heart. It was as if her hope was increasing along with the summer sun. For a brief moment, she realized she hadn't felt this sensation, hope, in a long time. This was surely a useful skill. She wondered how big a movement she could enact. Maybe she could tree-travel to Orlando, Florida and shake the ground right out from under Harmony Farms! Her mind began to turn with possibilities.

Gaia was dancing from one foot to another. "This is

wonderful! I was certain this would take all day to teach you! I knew you knew trees, but wasn't certain how you would fare with the soil."

The soil is in my blood, Gaia. Elizabeth thought. She felt her heart lift even more and her resolve solidify. She felt taller. She felt older. She truly would be able to save her farm; she was certain of it.

Gaia spoke. "I suggest you find a wide-open space away from the eyes of others. Practice. You must not only practice the skill, but practice precision. This is why I need you. I am too large for precision. Each time I have attempted to move a little, I hurt too many. I need your small eyes and precise attention. Do you understand?"

Elizabeth thought about how much more precise the third cell in her pinky toe would be working from the inside than she would be working on the outside. "I think so. Gaia?"

"Yes dear?"

"How do I reach you? How do I call for you if I need you?"

There was a long pause. Gaia's voice was lower and

somber when she answered. "It isn't so simple. I am not a god or a genie. I do not think there is a magic spell that conjures me here. Today I just felt it was time to come. I will say that throughout my whole being runs a song. It is the harmony of the whole earth. If you can learn to be in the song, you can be in a place to call to me. Do you understand? Just like the song of the aspen trees."

Elizabeth thought about the way Gaia's name had reverberated inside of her, like music, the first time she heard it. She thought about sitting on the porch the day before. *Ah! That's why Gaia came!* Maybe this was why she tended to hum little nothing songs and be filled with contentment each time she went into the garden or up to the woods. Had she always been aware of this song?

"I think so, Gaia. I will practice. I will save my farm."

"I know you will, dear. And, then you will help save me."

22
Love at First Strawberry

Gaia had left Elizabeth to her practice. Elizabeth decided to go to an open field that hadn't yet been cut for hay. While Maizey bounded back and forth, snout to the ground, chasing woodchucks back into their holes, Elizabeth practiced and it was great fun.

She moved hillocks of soil left and right, and up and down the field. It was funny to see the tall grasses and the Queen Anne's lace rising and falling in waves as if they were some strange terrestrial oceans. Red-winged blackbirds were startled up out of their nests and rose into the blue sky squawking and looking for intruders. Twice she popped a very surprised Maizey up high enough that she could see her big brown eyes go wide. It was great fun!

Elizabeth finally lay back in the tall grass. The sun had successfully pried apart the clouds and the day was warm. Elizabeth didn't mind the bit of dampness that pressed against her back because the sun on her face was pleasing. Maizey, tongue lolling and chest heaving, plopped down beside her and gave the woodchucks a break. Elizabeth watched the clouds rise and chase each other from hilltop to hilltop. She decided to relax and try to hear the song, the song of this field and this time.

The cottonwoods that bordered the field seemed to sigh and breathe. The blackbirds and swallows dipped and rose and called to each other. The grasses hissed in the breeze and their tasseled tops waved in unison. Elizabeth began to hear the song and the pattern. It was perfect. She smiled and nestled deeper into the grass. It was more restful than any bed and the song that enveloped her was more comforting than any down duvet that could ever be made. She slept.

Elizabeth did not know how long she had been asleep or what time it was. The sun was much further to the west and she knew it was time to get home. As she pulled her stiff legs up underneath her and rose up out of the grass, she heard the clanging of the big school bell. The bell was the call home and she and Maizey took off at a run. Normally, Elizabeth tried to keep up with the long stride of the Bernese mountain dog. She took three running steps and had a better idea. She dashed to the side of the field and flung her arms around a cottonwood tree. *Please, send me home to The Chaplain.*

Was it her imagination or was this whole tree travel thing getting easier? She actually was relaxed enough to enjoy the way the sound of the bell increased in volume as she drew closer. She arrived in a high crotch of the backyard oak and grinned "fit to split," as her father would say. This time, she waited until her mother went back inside before she began to climb down.

Maizey bounded up from the creek. Elizabeth called down, "Hey slowpoke! I finally beat you!" Maizey pulled up short under the tree and looked up at Elizabeth. She had never seen a dog looked surprised before. Maizey looked over her shoulder toward the creek and then back as Elizabeth dropped to the ground. Elizabeth laughed out loud. "Get used to it, you big oaf!"

When she came into the kitchen, dinner was on the table and her mother had already sat down. Her father's place was empty. "Where's Dad?"

Her mother released a long sigh. "He went to the school. There is a town meeting tonight to discuss the Harmony Farms' school proposal."

Elizabeth grabbed the bowl of green beans and dished them onto her plate. She loved the early beans; they tasted like the garden smelled, rich and full of life.

"Why do they want to waste money on a new school? Our school is fine."

Her mother set down her fork, but continued to look at her plate. "Well, your school isn't as fine as you think. I'm certain the electrical and plumbing are quite old and your computer lab is laughable, considering."

"Considering what?"

"Considering that the world revolves around computers, and today, knowing how to defrag your hard drive is as important as how to balance a checkbook! Look kiddo, we'll know more once your dad gets home."

"But why would people let Harmony Farms wreck everything?"

"Money. It's that simple. Most people have a price; they can be bought. And in a rural school district, like this one, it's unlikely that property taxes alone could ever support a whole new facility. Add to that all the jobs that Harmony Farms is creating, and it's a very tasty carrot dangling on the end of a stick, one that is sure to whack us in the end."

"Isn't money important? I mean, aren't things better, the more money you have?"

Her mother began clearing the table, but kept right on talking. "Listen, when I lived in New York (she was talking about the city) I had all the money one could want. I had a chauffeured car that took me anywhere I wanted to go. I had the best clothes, I ate at the best restaurants, and I knew the 'best' people." (She made little air quotation marks when she said "best people.") Only they weren't the best people. Most were people whose whole value system was based on the ability to consume."

"Were they fat?"

"Not that kind of consume!" She laughed and continued. "Their opinions of people were based on what kinds of things they bought; the more, the better, the more expensive, the better. I found it frustrating. Before I went into advertising, I studied art and thought about becoming an artist."

Elizabeth smiled. Her mom would've been a great artist. She had looked at her field journal enough to know that. She wondered why she didn't do it.

"It made me sad that for all the plays, operas and art exhibit openings I attended, I met very few people who actually gave a rat's behind about music, or art, or any creative endeavor."

Only she didn't say "rat's behind." She used a harsher word and Elizabeth was surprised because her mother rarely used any bad words. But there was color in her cheeks now, and Elizabeth could tell she was just getting started.

"What really started to get to me was that, not only had I chickened out at being an artist, but I was using my talents to create an appetite for useless stuff. The goal was always to get people to buy more and more stuff.

I talked to psychologists to understand what made people feel bad about themselves so that I could convince them that my client's product would make them feel good again. Advertising is a sick thing, Elizabeth. It isn't just about making you aware of what is available anymore. This is why I prefer the television stay off as much as possible. Advertising is about convincing you that you are flawed and that your salvation can be bought." She paused.

"Your father was my salvation." Elizabeth set her

chin in her hands and waited quietly. She loved the story of how her parents met, but this was the first time she had heard the word salvation used!

"Your father sat in that little farmers market with a grin fit to split his face! You inherited that grin, you know that?" She reached out and tickled a finger under Elizabeth's chin. Elizabeth laughed and thought it odd that in the midst of so many things that should feel so bad, she felt really good.

"Your father, whose truck was a rattling nightmare, whose clothes were plain and whose nails had never even heard of a manicure, had a light in his eyes that I rarely was privileged to see anywhere else in my fancy Manhattan world."

"It was the air and the water, right?" Elizabeth loved this part of the story!

Her mom was smiling, lost in the memory. "Yeah." she sighed. She suddenly snapped to attention. "Hey! You know the rest. Love at first strawberry; end of story. Now, daylight is a'wastin' and we have beans to pick! Get your chores done and I'll meet you between the rows!"

Elizabeth did her usual after-dinner duties. She took out the compost and as she scraped the food bits into the bin she swore she heard a teeny tiny "yum, yum, yum" kind of sound. But it was so faint she decided it was her imagination and the memory of those delicious beans!

She went to check on the saplings, and as she walked up and down the rows, she could vaguely hear the sighs and whispers and gentle singing of the young trees. A young plum tree and a dwarf apple actually reached down to tickle the back of her neck! She bid them all good night and then set off to the kitchen garden that sat on the west side of the house.

Her mother was on a short folding stool half hidden by the leaves of the bean plants. Elizabeth could hear the little *plop* sound of beans being tossed into the plastic basket. She grabbed her own stool and sat down at the opposite end of the long row. She hated the scratchy feel of the bean leaves, but loved the beans themselves. She picked and gathered a fistful and then got off her stool and headed down the row. After she dumped her fistful into the basket, she tapped her mother on the shoulder. Her mother looked up; sweat was beaded along her forehead.

"Tell me the rest of the story."

"You know the rest of the story."

"Please."

Her mother grinned, swiped the back of her hand along her forehead and said, "As long as you pick while you listen."

Elizabeth got back to her row and her mother began talking loudly, so that it carried down the row.

"Each week, I went to the farmers market on 77th Street and bought whatever was in season. I passed by your father's stand a number of weeks in a row, but didn't stop. Well, I couldn't help but notice that every person who stopped at his stand would laugh and smile and seem to walk away with a little more sunshine around them than when they came. Each time I walked past, he grinned and winked.

He finally stopped me to ask why I didn't ever stop at his stand. 'I see you looking over here, but you never come to sample my produce. Why is that?' he said to me and oh, did he have a devilish twinkle in his eye!

I saw his big display of strawberries and told him I didn't care for fruit that much. 'Ah!' he said. 'That is because the fruit you've had has not been grown from the richest soil and the purest water.' He held up a ripe red strawberry.

I don't know why I did it. I was never a very adventurous person. But I just had to know the secret of the twinkle in this man's eyes and it seemed like maybe the secret was in that strawberry. I closed my eyes and opened my mouth."

Elizabeth was picking much closer to her mother now. She tossed another handful into the basket and was practically holding her breath. This was the best part! Her mother continued, "He held it while I bit into the sweetest, juiciest strawberry I had ever tasted. 'Keep your eyes closed,' he whispered, and I did. As I chewed that bite of strawberry, I felt like my body came alive. I felt like I had tasted strawberries for the first time. I opened my eyes and saw that grin of his, stretched between the dimples and underlining the sparkles in his eyes. I knew."

"That it was love at first strawberry!" Elizabeth

finished for her.

Inside, her mother stood at the sink washing beans and humming. The telling of the tale had brought a little brightness back into her mother and it made Elizabeth eager to see her father. She decided to wait on the front steps for her father to get home.

23
Eminent Domain

Elizabeth and Maizey sat on the front steps in the waning light of the evening. Elizabeth twined her fingers in Maizey's long dark fur and thought about what makes a person rich. Robins laughed as they flitted back and forth across the circular drive. The pine trees that lined the drive dipped and swished their long needles and whispered to each other. Far off at the end of the drive, the top of The Sentry could be seen nodding along, as if in agreement with the pines that it was, finally, a great summer evening.

Elizabeth was picking bits of green bean out of her back teeth with her tongue and thinking that she wouldn't trade such a moment for a thousand, million dollars. She could hear the music: the way all the pieces of that evening were fitting together as they should. The low notes came from the ground drinking down yesterday's rain. Larks and sparrows and wrens provided the high notes. It also seemed that the clouds rushing eastward up the valley had a part in the symphony. Elizabeth didn't even pause to wonder at her ability to hear this song. She knew that somehow she had always heard it and that her time with Gaia had been like turning up the volume. She was getting used to it. But just as she was really picking up on this day's unique tune, the song started to become discordant.

It was as if the musicians were starting to play off

different sheets of music. The song of the evening was losing its rhythm and connectedness. Elizabeth looked around and was perplexed. What had changed? She heard the rumble of tires and gravel and knew: her father was home!

As her father barreled past the house and down to the barn, she caught a flash of his face and it was twisted and terrible. *Be brave.*

Mud spattered up behind the truck and he never turned to see Elizabeth and Maizey, waiting on the steps. She heard the bang of the back screen door and knew that her mother was going out to meet him. She started to get up to follow, but something caught her eye.

The stump of the cherry tree that now held perennial flowers was in the middle of the circular drive. Elizabeth walked toward it, wondering if tree stumps had the same capability as trees themselves. She sat down and grasped the edges of the stump with both hands. She pictured the saplings down by the greenhouse. She knew her father would be parking the pickup nearby.

Please, can you tell me what you hear? She felt a shudder leave her and move down and through the ground. She sat with her eyes closed tight and her lips pursed. She was just beginning to think that the tree stump wouldn't be able to help her when a new sensation began to fill her mind.

It was as if she were dropped down into the dark with a crowd of a million creatures all clamoring in chattering, indistinct voices. It reminded her of the teeny tiny "yum, yum" voices at the compost pile. She ran her mind from voice to voice until she could hear, moving closer, what seemed like giant deep voices, but she understood them. The sensation of movement stopped, and the big deep voices were above her. Not only could she hear them, but behind her eyes she began to see them.

"The whole town has gone crazy!" It was her father's voice and it was so filled with anger that it made dark blue-black swirls twist and move behind Elizabeth's eyes. "All anyone can talk about is the 'economic gain.' Harmony Farms has told the town council that time is an issue. They have this insane goal of slaughtering 7,000 hogs a day by Christmas! They said that they will help expedite the environmental impact study by supplying the surveyors themselves instead of the town having to go through an open bidding process!

Can you believe it? They're actually going to be over at the Danners tomorrow surveying. They want to be pouring cement in a month! So much for oversight! It stinks! The whole thing is rotten and I want to know who is getting paid off! I bet that John Winters is! That weasel!"

Elizabeth was surprised. John Winters was Rachel's father. He wasn't a weasel. He was a pretty nice guy. Her mother's voice came through and the swirling bruises that were her father's voice were pushed aside by what looked like soft green ribbons. "I'm sure that John isn't doing anything illegal. We have bylaws to govern development like this. What did Mayor Lawson say?"

"Oh, you'll love this one! Our fine Mayor said that when he met with Harmony Farms executives over dinner last month they assured him of the company's high standards of water and soil contamination controls. Dinner! LAST MONTH! Did you read anything about that in the paper? I sure didn't!" The angry black and blues swirled all remnants of the green ribbon away.

The green ribbon snaked back in. "Sweetie, bottom line, how will this affect us?"

"I'd like to tell you that it was only as bad as our well water being befouled, but it's worse Julia, much worse."

Elizabeth was fascinated. Before her father's voice even changed, she could see the swirls of dark blue and black beginning to fade. They were becoming a soft violet. The sadness in her father's voice revealed why.

"There was a map."

"I don't understand," the green ribbon replied.

"There was a map of the whole operation: the big metal barns, the slaughterhouse, and the office building. Julia, you are standing in the future office of the General Manager of Harmony Farms, NY."

There was a long pause. Elizabeth would have wondered if somehow she had lost the connection, except she could see the colors. The soft green ribbon started to sink and darken and also became an unhappy violet color.

"We aren't selling," her mother whispered. "They can't make us sell."

"It's called eminent domain. The town thinks they can make an eminent domain case because of the increased tax revenue and school improvements. They can make us sell. The town can.

When I said I would fight this and I wanted an attorney before discussing it further, I was booed right out of the room. It was awful, Julia. People I have known my whole life were looking at me like I was the enemy. Jack Forter even shook his fist at me. They have all gone crazy because they think their property taxes are going down and their salaries are going up."

Elizabeth watched as the purple swirls that were her father's voice turned a sick gray and sank from view. Her own stomach sank when she realized she could hear him sobbing. She forced herself to let go of the cherry stump.

She went inside and upstairs. She didn't want her

father to have to try to be cheerful in front of her. Seeing his red eyes and knowing that he had cried even while he smiled at her would probably make her scream. So she took Maizey, brushed her teeth, and went to bed.

When her mother poked her head in the door, Elizabeth simply said, "I got really sleepy waiting for Dad. Is he home?" There was a long silence. Elizabeth wondered if somehow her mother knew that she knew.

Her mother finally said simply, "He's home," and closed the door. And for the first time in her young life, nobody said, "I love you" before she fell asleep.

24
Laughter & Tears

Elizabeth knew what she had to do. She lay in her bed and ran scenarios through her mind of how the plan would work. She wouldn't need Gaia. She knew how to do this on her own. It was simple. Elizabeth heard what her father had said and when Harmony Farms came tomorrow, she would be waiting.

She wasn't sure when she fell asleep, but low whines from Maizey woke her up. "What is it, girl?" Suddenly her room was lit bright as day and then the night quickly clamped back down; a low rumble followed. Maizey had always been scared of thunderstorms. Elizabeth patted the bed and allowed the giant dog to jump up. It wasn't long before they were both hot and panting from the heat and the nervousness.

Together they watched the flashes and listened to the breaking open of the sky. Rain lashed the window and the oak tree outside was whipping its branches from side to side. *See, even the trees and the sky are angry,* Elizabeth thought, and eventually, she slept again.

The cooing of mourning doves and the smell of coffee wafting up the stairs pulled Elizabeth up to wakefulness. For the briefest moment, she wished it were just a normal day. When she turned onto her side and saw the Iroquois knife on her dresser, she sighed and pushed the wish away.

She washed and dressed, securing the knife to her ankle. *Today of all days, I must be brave. Today, I save our farm.*

Breakfast was as strange and silent as bedtime had been. Her mother kept looking out the window and her father kept his head down. He ate fast. When he finished, he glanced at Elizabeth and gave her a smile with his mouth only. His eyes were worried. Elizabeth could hardly believe her good fortune when her father did speak. "Good day for fishing, kiddo. The rain will have brought 'em up."

She had been wondering what reason she could give to be out along the creek all day and now her father had handed her one. "Can I, Mom?"

Her mother looked right through her a moment and then said, "I suppose. But I don't want you in the creek today. All this rain has it up too high, and we don't know if more fell upstream. And take Maizey with you. I don't want her tracking mud in all day."

Elizabeth packed a sandwich, a rain poncho, and bug spray into her backpack. She also ran into the office and grabbed the small binoculars off the windowsill. This was a stakeout after all. She kissed her mother on the cheek, whistled for Maizey, and headed outside.

They walked down the creekside path. Her mother was right. The creek was high. It was not giggling merrily to itself the way it usually did. It was boiling and jumping and seemed like it wanted to leap right out of its banks and get them. The willows were still dripping the morning's rain off their long branches. The day was warming quickly, and the moist earth was giving up the water in rising tendrils. Elizabeth thought it was funny the way the water was dripping down and rising up at the same time.

Because the creek curved to the south, it took about ten minutes before she was on Danner property. She broke away from the path and pushed through the underbrush toward the edge of a field. Maizey followed. "You couldn't go in front of me, you big ox?" Maizey didn't answer, unless panting counted.

At the edge of the field, Elizabeth had a clear view to the Danner house. Already, there were two extended cab pickup trucks in the driveway. They were bright yellow and bore the Harmony Farms logo on the side. After seeing pictures of the CAFO sheds and suffering pigs, seeing that happy red barn and silo made Elizabeth's jaw tense. "They're liars."

The Danner children swarmed around the Harmony Farms men. Even from this distance, Elizabeth could hear the squawk of their bickering. They sounded like a flock of angry chickens.

Elizabeth watched, wondering where they might begin their surveying. To her surprise, they hopped in their bright yellow trucks and came rumbling down a dirt road toward the creek. Elizabeth decided to stay where she was. Further down, there was little cover along the creek's edge. *Mr. Danner must cut and clear any brush and saplings. Typical.* It was what her father had talked about: using what Mother Nature gave. Brush at the edge of the field would have encouraged bug-eating birds to come. But Mr. Danner obviously preferred pesticides over birds.

Four of the Danner children came galloping along behind the Harmony Farms trucks. It looked like Dell, Debbie, Dave, and Don. Elizabeth could hear them shrieking at each other as they drew closer. She watched Debbie smack the back of Dell's head and Don kick out a foot to trip Dave. It seemed that a few weeks of summer vacation had done little to quiet the unruliness of the Danner kids. For a moment, Elizabeth imagined what it must be like to be stuck indoors on a rainy day at the Danners'. She shuddered at the image.

Maizey began to whine. Elizabeth decided to move further off the path and closer to the creek. She hunkered down under a holly bush and laced her hand through Maizey's collar. She wanted to be sure the big dog wouldn't give her away. She watched the men begin setting up tripods. They began to spread out and move apart. One of the men walked past Elizabeth's spot. She could hear the crackling of the voices coming through his walkie-talkie.

She realized that he was setting up along the tree line that separated her property from the Danners'. She hunkered down lower and commanded Maizey to lie down as well. She could still hear the Danner children yelling and carrying on when the idea came to her. She could do a repeat performance on Dell, except this time she knew what she was doing.

She lay flat on her belly and crawled forward until she could see down the length of the field. Maizey, because she was such a good dog, crawled right along beside her and lay panting. Elizabeth threaded one hand back through Maizey's collar, just in case, and placed her other palm flat on the ground. She took a deep breath and sent out a wave.

She couldn't have been more delighted with the results. The small ripple that she had sent along the field's edge knocked all four children off their feet as neatly as bowling pins. The howls and the accusations rose up. "You pushed me! Did not! I'm telling!" If they had sounded like angry chickens before, they now sounded like fighting roosters!

Elizabeth stifled a giggle and waited. The squabbling foursome were standing, brushing themselves off, poking and pinching and hurling insults at each other. The man from Harmony Farms hollered something at them and they moved around the front of his truck. They were now very close to the creek's edge.

Elizabeth decided to give them all another shove.

The thought went down, the ripple went out, and the Danners went down. Now they were mad as hornets! Elizabeth clamped her hand over her mouth and shook with stifled laughter.

She reminded herself that she was here to spy on Harmony Farms, not play 'bowling for Danners.' As her smile faded, she sensed something was wrong. She could feel a sort of shifting and shaking in the ground beneath her. She heard a loud yell and looked up in time to see the Harmony Farms man grab the back of Debbie Danner's shirt collar and give her a mighty yank. She flew back alongside the truck as the ground along the edge of the creek gave way and fell in with a large muddy splash.

It was like a hem unraveling. Dirt from the creek's bank continued falling. The loosening of the soil was running right along the bank. Elizabeth realized that she was on the bank! She started to push herself up when she was tugged over sideways by Maizey, who apparently also thought that it was time to skedaddle. Her hand was still snug through Maizey's collar and Maizey was trying to pull her through the underbrush.

The approaching collapse sounded like a roaring beast advancing on them. Elizabeth was just reaching up to free her hand when she felt the world fall away from under her!

They were in the creek and the creek was high and mighty! Maizey immediately began paddling and the motion dunked Elizabeth under the frothy, dirty water. The water was so swift and high that when Elizabeth first opened her eyes she saw, already about twenty yards behind her, the Harmony Farms truck slide down into the creek and begin a sickening slow roll onto its side.

Elizabeth sputtered the foamy water from her mouth and tried to figure out which way was up. Something kept poking and scratching her, and she couldn't seem to make her arms swim. Flashes of sky came and went and she heard something pounding and splashing the water near her head.

For a long moment her face remained out of the water. She realized that her hand was still tight in Maizey's collar. Maizey was trying her best to swim (that was the splashing), but they were both tangled in the holly bush that until a few moments ago had provided their cover.

The creek had its way with the bush. It turned it and pushed it and made it impossible for either her or Maizey to get their bearings. Elizabeth's ears filled with the sound of rushing water. It seemed each time she rose above water enough to see what was happening, Maizey was trapped below. When Elizabeth was trapped beneath the bouncing foam, Maizey furiously tried to paddle free on top.

They continued to spin and roll with the bush digging and grabbing at them. Each time Elizabeth went under, she went under with a smaller breath to sustain her. They were going to die if this continued. Elizabeth felt fear beginning to wind around her. It pressed in on her like a boa constrictor squeezing the life out of its prey. As soon as her mind labeled the sensation, "fear," she remembered that she had a tool to help her feel brave: the knife!

She reached down and began to dig at her pant leg. It was wet and wouldn't pull up easily. She dug and clawed and scraped until she felt the knife's handle.

She pulled it free, reached up, and began to saw at the nylon collar.

Halfway through, the dog and the collar went under again. Elizabeth sawed the blade even harder. Her arm burned. Her breath came in short gasps as the water sprayed into her face. The collar popped free so suddenly that Elizabeth's hand flew up. She saw the knife blade flash once as it turned in the air before both she and the knife went under.

She had both her arms now. She pulled for shore, but was so bone tired that the shore didn't seem to get any closer. She wanted to look around for Maizey, but was too tired to turn her head. She kept her eyes focused on the now unfamiliar shoreline and pulled. At last, her arms were reaching for the muddy slope and her feet were squishing in deep, soft mud.

She collapsed on the bank and turned her head. She saw the bush round the bend, but there was no big black nose poking out of the water. She pushed up and scanned the stream; Maizey was nowhere to be seen.

"Maizey!" Her first attempt at calling her friend came out as a wet rasp. She pulled up on her knees and coughed and spat out more water. She sat up on her knees and tried again.

"Maizey!" The only answer was the swirl and growl and gurgle of the creek.

She climbed up the slippery, muddy slope and found herself in an unfamiliar cornfield. She looked at the surrounding hills and judged that she must be close to where Sing Song Creek dumped into the Avon River. She was about two miles from home!

Elizabeth leaned against a poplar tree and tried to collect her thoughts. *How do I get home? Where is Maizey? What went wrong? Where is Maizey? I lost the knife! How do I tell Dad? Oh no! I have to tell him Maizey is lost in the creek! How do I get home?* She decided to look for Maizey first. There was nothing more important than the best friend she had ever had.

She followed the cornfield around the bend and sure enough, there was the broad, muddy delta where the creek opened out into the river. She had been here once before. Last summer, her father and she had draped themselves in old inner tubes and rode all the way down Sing Song Creek and then down the slow, wide river to town. When they had pulled out, her father bought her lunch at Gino's Diner and then they called her mother to come pick them up. It had been a great day.

Elizabeth remembered how excited she had been when they had reached the river. The sun had been shining hot, and Elizabeth had watched a great blue heron wading through the shallows, head cocked, looking for fish to spear. The Avon River had been a calm, dirty green color, slow and shallow, and on that day her heart had lifted at the sight of it.

In contrast, seeing the river now, her heart sank. The river was a rain-swollen beast. It had in its grasp all manner of trees and shrubs and miscellaneous garbage. She scanned the grey and foamy surface for anything that might be the large round head of the Bernese mountain dog. She called Maizey's name until her throat began to feel hot. She thought about how quickly the creek had carried her and Maizey to the river and she knew that Maizey could be miles from her by now. When her mind offered up the thought that she might never see her friend again, she turned and threw up creek water and scrambled eggs.

Throwing up seemed to drain the last of her energy; she fell to her knees in the mud. Elizabeth didn't know how long she knelt in the mud, head hanging, too tired to think or cry. A breeze began to pick up and, as if carried along on the wind, a song began to find its way into her ears. She heard the earth swallowing the water of the last two days. She heard small rabbits and woodchucks nibbling the soft, damp blades of grass. Gaia's song began to penetrate her exhaustion and grief.

Gaia. Gaia where are you? Why didn't you help me?

She thought this over and over and the thought seemed to fold itself into the song. She sensed another voice in the harmony of all that was around her. It was not the high sparkle that she had come to think of as Gaia's voice. It was a girl's voice.

Elizabeth opened her eyes. There, in the mud in front of her were two small feet. She looked up to see a girl with dark eyes, a wide face, and long black hair. She had a smile pulling the corners of her lips. Her eyes were shining. Elizabeth knew that look. It was the same look that Rachel had when she had been bursting with her Disney World news.

The strange girl brought her hands out from behind her back and there, impossibly, was her father's knife! Elizabeth felt her breath leave her. *Maybe I'm dead. Maybe I drowned and I am making all this up in my head. Who is she?*

It was then that she heard Gaia, her voice sounding like the rustle of leaves in the wind. "We did come to help. We helped you reach the shore."

Elizabeth looked past the smiling girl and saw the pointy snout of the otter bobbing in the angry water of the river. She felt something hot stirring in her belly, and it wasn't her scrambled eggs.

"You helped? You helped this happen!"

"No dear." Gaia said. "You did this. We just helped you out."

The girl bent down and laid the knife by Elizabeth's knees. She winked at Elizabeth and said in a soft voice that could barely be heard above the river, "Be brave!" Then she turned, walked to the river's edge and dove in! Elizabeth grabbed the knife and leapt to her feet. She scanned the water, but didn't see either the strange dark-skinned girl or Gaia. She finally knelt down to return the knife to her ankle.

I did this, Elizabeth thought. *Gaia said I did this. Maizey is gone because of me!*

She leaned up against a large sycamore tree and tried to cry. The tears never came. They seemed to sink downward into her body and form a cold, dark lump. She finally looked up at the sycamore's branches and the sunlight glinting off the shiny emerald leaves. She wrapped her arms around the sycamore and thought. *Please, oh please, send me home to The Chaplain.*

25
Lost

Elizabeth sat high in the branches of The Chaplain with two thoughts turning over in her mind. *I did this. I failed.* She could feel the mud drying on her skin, pulling it tight, and in places scratches and cuts began to feel warm. She ignored it all and kept turning those thoughts over in her mind.

The day grew hotter and more humid. The sun was now straight up and insects were buzzing insistently in the tall grass. As soon as Elizabeth became aware that she was starting to hear Gaia's song, she clamped her hands over her ears and said, "No. No. No," softly to herself over and over. She didn't want to hear it. She didn't want any part of it. She had failed.

Below her, she heard the phone in the kitchen ring. Her mother's muffled voice came through the open kitchen window.

"Hello? Yes. No, she isn't here; she went fishing."

There was a pause and then her mother's voice took on a high, panicked pitch.

"How? No, we haven't seen her!"

The back screen door banged open and her mother screamed out across the yard, "Daniel! Daniel!" She began to ring the school bell hard and fast.

Elizabeth started to understand and scrambled down the oak as fast as she knew how. When she dropped to the ground she looked up to see her mother, holding the screen door open with her foot, the phone in one hand and the school bell still waving in the other. Her mother paused for only an instant before she dropped both bell and phone and dashed down the steps.

She hugged Elizabeth so hard it hurt.

"I'm OK. I'm OK. Mom, I'm OK." She had to forcefully pull out of her mother's strong arms.

Her father and Will came running up the slope of the yard.

"What happened?" Her father's eyes were wide and his face pale.

"There's been a collapse. A big stretch of the creek bank over at the Danner's collapsed and people are hurt. One man is missing. Dell found Lizzy's backpack and they thought...they called...I thought..."

Her mother stopped to again squeeze her tightly. Elizabeth wrestled back out of her embrace. She had to tell her father.

"Dad, Maizey went in. I couldn't find her!"

He knelt down and clasped her shoulders. "Are you OK?"

"Dad, I'm fine, but Maizey is gone! Dad! I couldn't find her! I looked. I walked. I.." She couldn't finish her sentence. The cold ball of tears she carried in her belly made their way up and out of Elizabeth. Her vision became blurred, but through the prism of sadness she saw Will running down to the barn, and although the day was now heavy with heat, she started to shiver.

Her mother was saying they needed help at the Danners'. Will was running back up with hanks of rope over each shoulder. "C'mon!" was all he said, and he took off at a run down to the creek-side path. Her father looked at both of them quickly and then turned and ran as well.

Far off, the sound of sirens could be heard. They pierced the steam of the day and Elizabeth again had to clamp her hands over her ears. She didn't want to think about what the sirens meant. She didn't want to think about what she had done.

She barely remembered her mother taking her inside and getting her into a cool bath. She barely remembered lying on her bed while her mother put an antiseptic herbal balm on all her scratches. She didn't remember falling asleep. And, thankfully, in her sleep, she didn't remember or think or dream at all.

When Elizabeth woke it was dark. It was dark but still very hot. The night was heavy and pressing down on her sheet. In the distance a rumble of thunder rolled. The thunder seemed to say that something had happened and something was wrong. When she swung her legs off the side of the bed and there was no large fuzzy dog below, she remembered exactly what was wrong.

She sat on the edge of the bed with her head bowed. Below she could hear her mother on the phone, but chose not to try to understand what she said. When the screen door banged, she heard her mother say. "He's home. I'll call you back when I know."

She heard her parents talking in low voices for a while and then heard her father's big feet coming up the stairs. It sounded hollow and unreal to her. The door creaked open and his shape filled the doorway. Elizabeth smelled the sweat and the mud and the tiredness of him.

He stood there a little bit more before he said, "We

looked everywhere kiddo. We really did. We may never find Maizey." He waited a moment, probably hoping Elizabeth would say something, but she didn't.

"It could have been worse. Four of the Danner children were down there. One of Harmony Farms' men is still missing." Again he paused, waiting for a response from her.

Will said he'll go out to look again tomorrow. He's also going to put up notices in town in case she swam out and someone found her. I'm grateful you're OK. Get some sleep. Things will be better in the morning."

He closed the door and Elizabeth lay back down. How could things be better in the morning? The only way anything could be better was if Maizey came home.

26
Secrets

They didn't find Maizey, but they did find the Harmony Farms man. He was found clinging to the bushes near the bend in the creek right before the river. His name was Mervin T. Shott. He was an engineer and lived in Kissimmee, Florida. That is what Elizabeth saw in the newspaper.

The newspaper also talked about the future of Harmony Farms in Avon. The mayor said repeatedly that this kind of wet summer was rare and that it was most likely Mr. Danner's 'agricultural practices' that had made the bottomland unstable. Even in print he sounded nervous.

Elizabeth's parents spent more and more time in the office. Her mother spent more hours hunched over her computer keyboard with her brows knitted in concentration than she spent out in the garden with her eyes squinting against the sun. Elizabeth noticed that binders appeared on the desk with words like "CAFO Research" and "Fighting Eminent Domain" on the spines.

Elizabeth spent most of the next week sitting high in the platform of The Scout. It was the one place she was used to being without Maizey. It was the one place that still seemed normal. Will had strung a tarp over the platform so that even when the rain came pattering down through the leaves, Elizabeth could sit. It seemed the gray skies and the rain of that horrible damp summer were merely a reflection of what Elizabeth was feeling inside: cold, gray and tired.

Elizabeth didn't go looking for Gaia. She continually told her ears to ignore the green song around her. She had failed. She wasn't worthy of any gift that Gaia may be able to give her. She also felt she wasn't worthy of the gift her father had given her.

Late one evening when her parents had left the office and were on the back porch talking in low voices, she had taken the old knife and put it on top of her father's desk. She didn't need to be brave anymore. She just had to wait. It seemed that soon the sadness of that summer would be complete. She had heard her parents talking about moving to New York City.

She had only received one e-mail from Rachel. Her new email address was 'sunnyone@centralfl.com' Elizabeth felt mad just seeing that name. Here she was, suffering day after gray day, not able to swim or anything and Rachel was 'sunnyone.' The email had been stupid. Rachel talked about the big school she would be going to and the big mall nearby and the big stadium where her father had season tickets to see the Orlando Jazz play basketball. Big deal, Elizabeth thought. She didn't even ask one question about how I am.

She thought long and hard about how to respond. Should she tell her about how her father's new employer was making everyone in the town mad at each other? Should she tell her that the Danners had left and already the west wind smelled better? Should she tell her about Maizey? In the end, she did what was always most comfortable for her. She didn't say much. She hit "reply" and typed, "I am happy that you like your new town." She didn't sign her name. She didn't write BFF (best friends forever), the way she always had on the notes they had passed at school. She just hit the "send" button and felt that Rachel was as gone as Maizey.

One gray day followed another. It seemed the only birdsong that her ears picked up on was the Ha-Ha-Ha! of big black crows that didn't seem to mind the rain. They seemed to be laughing at her, as if they knew that she had failed and that soon the valley would be full of pig remains that they could feast on. Elizabeth had seen enough crows happily hopping out onto the road to pick at flattened woodchucks to know that they were not picky about their food. Ha-Ha-Ha! They looked at her with their black eyes and laughed in the midst of what felt like endless gray, sad days.

One afternoon, when the sun managed to beat out the rain clouds, Elizabeth sat up in The Scout and hummed an odd, discordant tune. It helped keep her ears from picking up any of the rising rhythm of that fine sunny day. It was hot enough for her to consider dipping her toes into the creek. But she quickly pushed thoughts of the creek from her mind. She might see Gaia there. If she went to the creek, she would have to think again about that scary, awful day in July. She slapped at mosquitoes and tried to pay attention to the book she was reading, *The Tale of Despereaux.*

"Hey there Lizard!"

Will's voice from the base of the tree made her jump. He came climbing up and shucked a small back-pack off.

"I come bearing gifts!"

He proceeded to pull out egg salad sandwiches wrapped in wax paper, a chessboard, and a large freezer bag filled with chess pieces.

"Today you finish learning this game, Lizzy."

"Can't you see that I'm reading?" Elizabeth bent back down over her book, although she wasn't really looking at the words anymore, just waiting to see what Will would do.

Will didn't do anything for a while. He sat and swung his legs over the edge of the platform. He finally spoke.

"It is pretty cool how you can see your whole farm from here."

Elizabeth didn't say anything, just scowled and continued to stare at her book. She didn't want Will's cheeriness invading her dark mood.

"I mean there's your mom, weeding that big garden of hers. There's your dad, cutting hay. And here you are, reading a book."

Elizabeth let those words sink in. Her cheeks felt hot and she could feel her heart begin to beat faster. She slammed her book and turned to face his back.

"What is that supposed to mean?"

"It means whatever you think it means." He turned and looked over his shoulder at her. He smiled a small, sad sort of smile. "I'm just worried about you Lizzy. I haven't seen you much and I don't think I've heard you laugh since the last day of school."

"There hasn't been a lot to laugh about. In case you hadn't heard, there are people who want to take Three Oaks out from under us. We might have to go live in the big stinkin' city while people like you stay here to run a big stinkin' pig farm. All so a bunch of guys who don't even live here can make more money!"

She was surprised to find that she was on her feet with her fists balled up at her sides and her jaw clenched so hard it made her temples throb.

"Whoa! Easy Lizzy! I came up here to see my friend, not do battle."

Elizabeth stepped back so that her back was against the broad trunk of The Scout. She didn't know why she did what she did next. Maybe it was because carrying a secret is the most tiring thing in the world. Maybe it was because, since both Rachel and Maizey were gone, she no longer had a best friend. Maybe it was just because. She smiled at Will and said, "You can have your stinkin' big pig farm. I'm leaving."

She closed her eyes and silently asked to be sent to The Sentry. There was a moment where nothing happened and she wondered if Gaia had found some other girl to help her out. But then came the familiar tugging and pulling and woody darkness.

She emerged, standing above the Three Oaks sign out by the main road. She looked up to the ridge of the hill and began to laugh. It was the first time she had heard her own laugh in a long time. She imagined what Will's face looked like and laughed harder. She laughed so hard that it shook tears from her eyes. She laughed because at least someone else would now know what she had done.

27
Will Knows

Elizabeth made it her business to avoid Will for the
next few days. She wasn't ready to talk to him, but she
did feel a great relief. The earth, too, seemed to have a
kind of release from the sodden gray weather that had

dominated the summer. The skies were a fierce blue and the few clouds that dared show their faces were high and thin and moving fast.

Elizabeth started to again visit the tree nursery. She began to allow her ears to open to the eager but shy songs of the young trees. She watered them and all the while missed Maizey. Mushrooms pushed up through the warm, wet soil of the sheep pasture and as she went out mornings to search for them, she missed Maizey. But she also began to feel a hint of the greater song stirring within. Out in the garden, as she weeded between the fragrant tomato plants, she felt the greenness of her surroundings feeding her a kind of strength. When she paused at the ends of the rows to turn her face up to the sun, her back felt strong and she began to miss the feeling of the knife at her ankle.

In the back of her mind a thought began to grow. Like an insistent little seedling, the thought pushed its way up through her mind and finally emerged bright and full of life. *What else was Gaia going to teach me? Maybe there is still a chance.*

Elizabeth had reason to reach for another chance.

She had watched as her mother held meetings in their living room with the Jeffries and the Volgels and other farm families that didn't want to sell. She had watched a series of cars and trucks with the lying logo of Harmony Farms park in front of the house. She watched the men in suits coming into the house all smiles and leave scowling and muttering about ignorant farmers.

She had heard the angry voices coming from behind the closed door of the office. It was those moments, more than any other, she wished Maizey had been there, to bark at them and make them feel afraid. Maizey had always barked if someone yelled in anger. If Elizabeth had to feel afraid, she thought it only fair that the Harmony Farms men be a little afraid too.

One Saturday morning, Elizabeth was dying skeins of wool in bilberry dye for her mother. Her back was to the door, but when she felt the hair on the back of her neck rise up, she turned to look. There was Will, leaning in the doorway, smirking.

"Sooooo, Lizzy the magician! I have you cornered,

and you have some questions to answer."

Indeed, he had her cornered. She was up to her elbows in purple, sudsy water and his tall frame filled the only doorway out of the washroom. She turned, pulled off her rubber gloves with a snap, and planted her hands on her hips. She didn't say anything because she was still the kind of girl who didn't speak unless she knew exactly what she was going to say, and she had absolutely no idea what she was going to say.

"Are you going to tell me how it is I watched a tree swallow you up and yet, here you are humming a merry tune as if nothing happened?"

Elizabeth hands fell from her hips. Had she been humming a merry tune? She realized that her ears were indeed, full of the music of the day. She laughed, rushed at Will, and threw her arms around him.

"Whoa! Whoa! I don't understand!"

Elizabeth jumped back and began to talk in a rush. She told him about the night she and Maizey first saw Gaia. She told him about knocking over Dell at school. She told him about the fairy ring. She told him about making Rachel mad by moving from the tree house to the plum tree. She was about to tell him about the day when the surveyors came, but stopped herself.

Will took a step through the doorway. His head was tilted and he had a strange look in his eyes.

"Lizzy, are you sure you haven't been staying up too late reading fantastical books?"

"Will, I swear it's all true. I don't want it to be true because...." Her voice seemed tangled in her throat. When she spoke next, she didn't feel real. She felt like she was watching a movie of herself talking. "Because if it is true, it means I'm the one that made the bank collapse at the Danners'. That was because of me."

Now that she had said it out loud, she felt the rest of the burden lift from her shoulders. There. Now she would see if Will really was her friend or just a rent-a-son from over the hill.

"Lizzy, that was an accident. There had been too much rain and the bank just washed out."

"No, Will. I did that. I did it. I tried to play a joke on Dell Danner. I made the bank crumble. Maybe it kept going because I was mad at Harmony Farms. I just didn't know how to make it stop. I didn't want that truck to fall in! I didn't mean for any of it to happen. I didn't know."

She hung her head and waited. Would she hear the slam of the washroom door? Would she hear his voice calling for her father? She trembled a little, deep in her belly. She didn't think she could bear to lose another friend.

He cleared his throat. "Lizzy, you have to go find Gaia. You have to find out what else you can do."

She lifted her head and saw that he was smiling down at her. In fact, he was smiling so big it made his eyes crinkle up.

"You don't think I'm crazy? You don't think I'm a bad person?" she whispered.

"Lizzy, I just came back from four days at one of Harmony Farms Incorporated 'farms' (he made little quote marks in the air when he said it). I think you are one of the good guys. I don't know exactly what you mean when you talk about pinky toes and green songs and such, but I know that if you're trying to keep our beautiful valleys from smelling foul, and if you're trying to keep the water clear and blue, and if you're trying to keep the air full of birdsong instead of the wretched screaming of hogs that I heard, then you, Elizabeth Angier, you are definitely one of the good guys."

Elizabeth again rushed forward and threw her wet arms around his skinny waist. She felt solid and safe again. She felt her heart lift with hope. She stepped back and looked at him.

"You were at one of their big pig farms?"

Will shook his head and looked at the floor. "Lizzy, I don't care if they paid me a hundred thousand dollars. I am a farmer, and what they're doing is not farming. They call the hogs 'units' and they have figured out that if you allot each 'unit' 8 square feet, they will bite and maim each other, but not kill each other. I have never seen such miserable animals. And at the slaughterhouse, the people are just as miserable. They 'disassemble' (again he used the air quotes) 7,000 hogs a day. It's a stinking, bloody mess that they can't begin to clean up during the night shift. It is the most disgusting thing I have ever seen. It's going to be a long time before I can eat pork again and when I do, you can bet I will go to Ivan the Terrible's for it."

Elizabeth thought of Ivan Sorsky who owned a tiny little farm on the other side of Avon. He had a handful of pigs, an old goat named Francis, and a lot of cats. He earned the name Ivan the Terrible because he always yelled at the kids who cut across his property when they walked home from school.

Will let out a hoarse laugh. "I can't believe we ever called him that. His pigs live a life of luxury compared to what I saw. Heck, even the Danner hogs were happier! That is why I have to believe you, Lizzy. I can't stand by and watch such misery come here. I've lived here my whole life and I want to keep living here, but who can live with Harmony Farms?" He lowered his voice and motioned Elizabeth closer. "I know what their plans are. I can help you."

Elizabeth also lowered her voice. "It might take me a few days to find Gaia. What can you do?"

"I was going to tell them to take their 'management job' (again he made the air quotes) and shove it up their snouts, but I guess I can play along for a while. I can find out all the details: timelines, site plans, things like that."

Elizabeth started pulling on her purple rubber gloves. As she turned back to the wash bin she said, "Will, you are my hero!"

"No Lizzy, you're our hero, even if no one ever knows it."

She turned her head over her shoulder to watch his back recede into the gloom of the lower barn floor. She turned back to the task of pulling the long strands of yarn through the purple, fragrant water and began to hum. She hummed along with the song that came up through the floor and in through the window. She hummed along to the high melody of larks, finches, and grosbeaks that were flitting back and forth. She hummed along with the gurgling of Sing Song Creek coming through the window. She hummed and whenever the space was there, she thought, *Gaia, please come. Gaia, I need you and you need me. Gaia. Gaia. Gaia.*

28
Be Brave II

Elizabeth spent the next day and a half anxiously watching the creek. Four or five times she walked along the ravine, starting where the trickle of water spilled into Sing Song Creek and then upwards through the sloping sheep pasture and into the dark shade of the woods. Her eyes strained for the sleek brown shape of Gaia. She stopped at one of the 'Tree T.V.' fallen trees and saw that the wet summer had changed things a lot. There were now many more salamanders scurrying to and fro and some kind of tiny frog that she had never seen before.

Normally she would have spent much more time examining the new developments, but her own entertainment took a back seat to what needed to be done. She left the log and went higher in the woods and up into the platform of The Scout.

To the west of Three Oaks, strange equipment and machinery began to arrive. From her perch, Elizabeth could see the bright yellow of ground moving and construction equipment pulling into the Danner farm. She decided it was time to suck it up and head back to the scene of her great failure. If she was going to ever help Gaia, she knew she had to rethink her failure. Mrs. Foster had always told the class that mistakes were "learning opportunities" and that you only failed if you didn't learn something from each mistake.

She went back down to the house to grab a plum from the fruit bowl. Surveillance was hungry work, after all! As she turned from the kitchen counter her feet seemed to freeze. She stared down at the deep blue/purple of the plum. Again, she was feeling a deep ache in her body where her love of Maizey used to be. *How can I go back? Maybe somehow the ground will know it's me, and finish the job.* Her mouth filled with the memory of the muddy creek water. Her ears filled with of the sound of rushing water. Worst of all, in her mind's eye, she could see Maizey's wide head, big black nose, and the thickness and texture of her red nylon collar, right before Elizabeth had cut it off to free her own hand.

She closed her eyes against the memory. She squeezed her eyes against the tears. A warm wetness shook her from the memory. She had squeezed the plum, and the wet, juicy flesh of it was now oozing from her hand onto the kitchen floor. It seemed to snap her out of her memory hole. She quickly cleaned the mess from her hand and the floor and headed to the office.

Her father sat at his desk on the phone and her mother was at the computer. They both had strained looks etched into their brows. They looked tired and older. The printer hummed with what Elizabeth assumed would be the contents of yet another binder. Her father gave her a quick glance and then closed his eyes to better concentrate on the conversation he was having. Elizabeth sat on the leather sofa and waited.

"You don't say. Mmmm. Mmmm." her father said. Elizabeth always hated hearing one side of a conversation. It made her mind ache to hear the other half!

"What did the tests show? What about the EPA report? Were they fined? Mmmm. Mmmmm. So you are willing to come up here and present this at our next town council meeting? Excellent! My wife, Julia, is e-mailing you the directions now. Mr. Sorjeson, I am grateful, absolutely grateful for your help. We are fighting for our lives here, and it's nice to know we aren't alone. Mmmm. Mmmm. Thank you again, sir. I look forward to meeting you Tuesday."

He hung up the phone and turned to Elizabeth with a smile. It was the first one Elizabeth had seen in a long time. She had never realized what a happy family she was living in until this horrible summer had started. She made a mental note to never forget this fact.

"Hey there kiddo! We have company coming!"

"Who?"

"Frank Sorjeson. He is a farmer from North Carolina. He lives next to the Harmony Farms operation and..."

"The one that Will visited?" she blurted.

Her father stopped his explanation of the impending guest. "Will went to North Carolina?"

Elizabeth pulled her lips in and squeezed them. She shouldn't have said anything. Her father obviously didn't know that Will had gone. She didn't want her father to think Will was the enemy or maybe he wouldn't be allowed around the farm anymore.

"Julia, did you hear that? Will Jeffries went to the Harmony Farms operation in North Carolina. You don't think he is taking a job with them do you?"

Her mother spun in her chair and looked over the top of her reading glasses at him. "You don't think Will can make a living on what we pay him, do you?"

"But…"

"You don't think that Will can just live at home forever and not want to build his own life, do you?"

"But…"

"Relax. Will told me all about his trip, and he said that there is no way he would ever work for that company or one like it. I'm just pointing out that this is the kind of argument we are up against. People want more predictability and more income than they currently have. You have to be prepared for that."

She turned back to her computer and continued clicking the keys rapidly. Elizabeth was always amazed that she could type so fast.

"Dad, I actually came in here to get something from your desk."

"Ah, I wondered if you would be back for it."

He turned to the big rolltop and pulled open a drawer and drew out the knife and sheath. He held it out to her. "I have to admit, I was sad when I saw it here. Why did you bring it back?"

She held the knife and stared down at it. She didn't want to blurt out something that would prevent her from being able to go back down to the creek again. She thought again about the dark day in the creek.

"I..I.." She almost faltered completely, but then in a rush she told him. "My hand was caught in Maizey's collar. I couldn't swim, I couldn't breathe! I had to cut it off! Oh Dad! I had to cut it off, and then I didn't see her again!"

Before she had even finished her last sentence, her father had swept her up onto his lap, something he hadn't done for a few years. She buried her face against his cotton tee-shirt and again squeezed her eyes against the tears. She gripped the knife even tighter. The time for tears was over. Now that she had Will on her side, it was time to fight for what was right.

She sat up and her father looked at her with big, sad eyes. "I had no idea. Sweetie, you did the right thing. I'm sure Maizey knows that."

Her mother came over and was stroking Elizabeth's back. "We're proud of you for making such a hard choice."

Her father let out a short laugh. "I'm proud of you for managing to hang onto the knife!"

Elizabeth remembered seeing it glint against the sky as her hand flew up and released it. It was only because of Gaia that the knife was still here: Gaia and the strange dark-skinned girl. Maybe it was only because of Gaia and the girl that she was still here. She allowed herself the quick, miserable thought. *I wish they had kept Maizey here too.*

She slid off her father's lap and smiled. "I'm looking forward to meeting Mr. Sorjeson. I've got work to do." She turned on her heel and headed toward the office door.

"What work do you have to do, kiddo?"

Elizabeth turned back and smiled at her parents. "It's a surprise."

29
Gaia Girl

Elizabeth made her way down to the bridge over Sing Song Creek. She paused at her favorite reading tree and leaned into the familiar smell and feel of the bark. She smiled. She had missed the energy of the creek. In some way she felt that her heart was finally starting to beat again. Now that it was back to being her sparkling, bubbling friend and not the dashing and dangerous beast it had been earlier in the summer, Elizabeth wished she had spent a little more time among the willows.

She made her way down the familiar creekside path. Up ahead, hidden by the bend in the stream, came a terrific tearing, crunching sound. She could feel a vibration in her feet and corresponding with it, the sound of a revving diesel engine. When she rounded the bend and stepped past the tree line that marked the division between Three Oaks and the Danners', she stopped still in her tracks. She now knew why deer would stop still in front of a moving car. Terror.

Across the field she saw two large yellow claw-like machines reaching high into the sky, one grabbing onto the roof of the Danner house, the other clasping the roof of the Danner barn. With a growl and a belch of smoke, they pulled. The sound of tearing, rending wood was terrific. It looked like the machines were eating the buildings. Elizabeth was horrified, but fascinated. She had never seen something so large being destroyed before.

"Hey Lizard Breath!"

Elizabeth crouched and spun, hand already to her ankle, seeking the bravery of her knife.

"Whoa up there, Lizzy!" It was Will and he had a terrific smirk plastered across his face. Elizabeth turned back toward the scene unfolding in front of her.

"I thought you might be down here," he said. "Weird, isn't it?"

"It is weird. I always hated Dell Danner, but now I wish he were here."

"I know. But it says something the way Mr. Danner happily sold out his family farm, took the money and split, while your dad continues to fight tooth and nail."

"The soil is in our blood," Elizabeth whispered to herself.

"What?" Will asked.

"Nothing. Something my great grandmother used to say." Even from this distance, the Harmony Farms logo seemed to mock her with its lying, cheery colors. "So! How do we stop these guys?"

"If what you said is true, if you can really move the dirt around, I think we can make this whole project too expensive for them to complete. But Lizzy," he turned and placed his hands on her shoulders. "You have to be certain, absolutely certain, you know what you're doing. We can't hurt anybody."

Elizabeth swallowed hard. "I'm waiting for Gaia. I need to know why things went so wrong before. I just know that I am missing something. I have to learn more."

They stood and watched a while more. The Danner farm was soon nothing but a few large piles of wood and shingles and a lot of muddy tracks in the ground. A backhoe was loading the piles into a string of dump trucks, which in turn, rattled off down the Danner's drive and went to some unknown place. Elizabeth wondered for a moment what unknown place Dell and Debbie and the rest of the Danners had gone to.

"I gotta run, Lizard Breath. Go find this Gaia girl."

"She's not a girl, she's an otter."

"OK, then *you* are the Gaia Girl. Call me or pop into one of my trees after you've talked to her."

Elizabeth smiled. *Gaia Girl*. She liked the sound of it, like a superhero. She could imagine a cape flapping at her shoulders with a big, green double G on the back.

"Can you do that tree thing again? Just so I know you aren't a liar and I'm not crazy."

Elizabeth's smile grew broader and she made a movement as if swishing a cape back off of her shoulders as she stepped toward the beech tree at the Three Oaks property line. She leaned against it and reached her hands back to feel the bark. She made certain to keep her eyes locked with Will's as she asked the beech to send her home to The Chaplain. The last she saw of Will, his grin was nearly splitting his face in half. The last thing she heard was Will cheering, "You go, Gaia Girl!"

30
Listen

The next day Elizabeth and her mother spent the entire morning clearing all the vegetable beds of the weeds that had taken advantage of the long days of rain. The sun beat hot on their backs and sweat ran down their faces, but Elizabeth didn't mind. After the cold, wet of June and July, it felt as if these later days of August were baking the sad ache from her. She hummed little songs to the plants and admired the way all the seeds she had so carefully planted in the spring were now colorful vegetables fit for the high-priced restaurants of New York City.

She reached the end of the row of broccoli and stood to stretch her back. *Done!* she thought, and the stand of paper birch trees before her began to applaud. The leaves clapped and spun although there was no discernable breeze. Elizabeth took a bow. *Thank you. Thank you. For my next trick, I will weed the potatoes!*

She had just settled into her comfortable weeding crouch when she heard a high, sparkling laugh. She looked around. Her mother's bent back could be seen three rows over. Again, Elizabeth heard the laugh that sounded like a thousand crystal bells chiming in the breeze. Without saying anything to her mother, she took off at a run toward Sing Song Creek.

When she reached the bridge, she again heard the laughter and now she could tell that it came from high up in the sheep pasture, along the ravine, where she had first met Gaia. She pumped her knees and arms and ran up as fast as she could. There at the edge of the woods was the long, sleek shape, standing on her back legs and waving one wee paw at her.

Elizabeth drew up, panting. "Finally! Finally! Oh Gaia, I am so sorry. I don't know what I did and then I was so mad, so mad that I didn't even want to listen to your songs anymore." She folded her legs and dropped to the ground.

Gaia also dropped back to all fours. Her dark eyes glittered and her whiskers twitched a few times. "Now you know. Now you know how it feels to try to do good and instead, cause pain." Elizabeth looked down at the clover of the sheep pasture. She thought about the Harmony Farms man. She thought about Maizey.

"I gave you some of my power," Gaia continued. "Now you have to learn what I have learned. I had to learn how to go very small and deep and focused in order to speak to you. Now you have to learn how to go very deep and very focused. Remember your pinky toe?"

"Yes."

"Well, it will not do either of us any good for you to talk to the fifth cell in your pinky toe, but the challenge is just as great. You have to learn to talk to, and to work with, the living parts of the earth."

"What do you mean, the living parts?" Elizabeth asked.

"I mean, just as there are things living inside of you that make your body run, there are millions and millions of creatures in a square foot of earth. They are the transformers. They are the ones who create my very flesh. It has been hard enough for me to concentrate enough to talk to you. I cannot speak to them."

"Transformers? I don't understand."

"In this case, dear, neither do I. I simply know what I feel. There are places where these transformers cannot exist anymore, and it is there that my very flesh begins to die. I do not understand completely how they work, but I can feel their work. This is one of the reasons I sought you out. Your home is dense and ripe with transformers. There are so many that they should make a lot of noise for you to listen to."

Elizabeth was silent, but her mind went back to the day her father had driven in, angry, from the town meeting. The day she had placed her hands on the cherry stump, but had heard and passed among a thousand small chattering voices before hearing her parents. Could those have been the transformers? Hearing the question in her mind reminded her that she had other questions for Gaia.

"Gaia, why did the creek bank fall that day? Why couldn't I stop it?"

"That place is one of the dead places." Gaia's voice sounded like the quiet sad call of the mourning dove. "There is hardly any life left in that earth. You could not control what you had started. In order to have control, you need to be connected into the life in the soil."

Elizabeth thought about Mr. Danner spraying pesticides all across his fields several times a season. She recalled her father saying, "Doesn't he know he is killing all the good with the bad? If he just left it alone, the good would take care of the bad on its own!"

"I think I understand." Elizabeth wasn't sure, but she was confident that she now knew where to explore next.

Gaia waddled to her and placed her dark paws on Elizabeth's knees. Her twitching black nose was inches from her face. Her black eyes seemed to hold the glitter of starlight. Her voice came out soft, like the softest breeze that ever caressed the trees. "I know you have been calling me. The reason I took so long was that I was bringing a surprise. Listen."

Listen. Listen. Listen. Elizabeth closed her eyes and quickly picked up on the ballad of the hot summer day. Punctuating the tune came a series of loud, demanding, familiar sounds. Barking!

Elizabeth's eyes flew open in time to see a great black shape barrel into her. She rolled back and down the hill and could hardly gather her mind around what was happening. A big pink tongue and hot dog breath smothered her face. Shaggy, dirty, black fur filled her vision.

"Maizey! Maizey! Maizey!" She heard herself crying over and over.

When she sat up to thank Gaia, the otter was gone. Maizey was wiggling and skipping like a puppy, but looked old and haggard. Her fur was matted and full of burdocks. She was thin and one ear had a ragged and crusted tear in it. Elizabeth didn't care. Maizey was alive and here at Three Oaks. She threw her arms around her again.

She rose and Maizey barked loud and fast. Down below, Elizabeth saw her father's shape come around the side of the barn. Even from this great distance, she could see the round circle of his surprised mouth. Together, Maizey and Elizabeth ran down to meet him.

31
The Stinky Visitor

Her father took Maizey to the vet the next morning. Her fur had to be cut short in a few places and shaven on her hip where a long, thin cut had to be cleaned. But they had bathed her and the vet reported good news.

Her father handed Elizabeth a green pill bottle.

"The vet said you have to give her two of these pills three times a day to keep any of those cuts from becoming more infected. You are also to keep the ear clean and get to work on fattening her back up! Can you handle that, kiddo?"

Elizabeth nodded. She would do anything to keep Maizey with her. That afternoon found the two old friends lying in the sun next to the bed of lavender. Elizabeth knew the scent of the herb was healing. She figured if it was good for people, it must be good for dogs too. Maizey lay, stretched out in a deep sleep. Elizabeth lay next to the great dog and occasionally waved her hand to keep the flies from landing on the injured ear or hip.

Elizabeth had her ear to the ground and decided it was as good a time as any to go meet "the transformers" Gaia had spoken of. She closed her eyes and sent her attention to the earth beneath her. Slowly, she began to perceive.

First she began to hear their activity. It reminded her of the tearing and crunching of the machines that had torn down the Danner's buildings. But this tearing was different. She sensed that they were breaking apart the leaves that had fallen, the grass clippings, the tiny lavender buds, and the many tiny parts of many tiny creatures that had lived and died without Elizabeth ever being aware of them.

She sank deeper still and perceived more. This was a whole miniature-farming world. Some creatures excreted things that made the plants above happy. Some creatures were able to crush even the smallest remains of things that had once been alive, until all that was left were the building blocks themselves. Elizabeth was enchanted. There were millions and millions of such creatures just in this small space of side lawn and herb garden in the sun. They were, in a way, the very texture and life of the soil.

She wasn't sure when she fell asleep, but she awoke when she felt Maizey jump up. She ran to the front of the house barking, and Elizabeth heard the crunching of tires coming up the lane. She heard her mother ring the school bell a few times, to call her father in. Elizabeth went to the front of the house and watched the station wagon pull around the circular drive.

A short, heavy, white-haired man pulled himself from the front seat. Elizabeth knew he was nice because Maizey was greeting him with a wagging tail and a big panting smile. Maizey always knew who to be friendly to. Her father came bounding out the front door.

"Welcome! Welcome, Mr. Sorjeson! I am so happy to have you here."

"I'm happy to try to help, but I'm also here to caution you on what you can realistically expect," the man said.

Elizabeth caught a funny smell, like the smell that used to come from the Danners' farm on days when the wind blew from the west. She wrinkled her nose. The man caught her eye and leaned down.

"It smells pretty bad, eh? My whole house smells this way. My whole family smells this way. Sometimes it is so bad that we wake up at night, gagging."

There was a big heavy silence as the Angier family let such a statement sink in. Was this the future at Three Oaks? Even if they could fight against being forced off their land to make room for an office building, would staying here mean waking up at night gagging on the smell of tens of thousands of unhappy hogs?

The Jeffries came to eat dinner with them that night. They all listened in mounting dismay as Mr. Sorjenson described the ongoing series of legal battles he and other people in his town had undertaken in an effort to get Harmony Farms to scale down, clean up, or move out.

"Y'all can't imagine what it's like to wake up every day of the summer with your windows black with flies. We have huge swarms of them coming from that CAFO. And if that weren't enough, most of our friends have to buy bottled water now; the runoff has tainted just 'bout every stream and well around it."

He looked around at their still faces. "Hey, don't look so glum! We've started to get some other organizations to help with this fight. We are suing to force the EPA to enforce the Clean Water Act. See, them fat cats in Washington don't want to enforce their very own laws because companies like Harmony Farms will cry

'Reduced profits' and give 'em less money on their next campaign."

Her mother was shaking her head. She sighed and said, "I can't believe I once was proud of an ad campaign I did for Chippy Chicken. If I had known then, what I know now." She didn't have to finish her thought. Everyone at the table was probably thinking about how the chickens at Chippy Chicken farms had to live.

Mr. Sorjenson sat his wide frame back in his chair and wiped his mouth with his napkin. "Now that's just 'bout what everyone says. I think part of what we need in the country is to get folks to 'member where their food comes from. We need 'em to care a little bit 'bout the pigs they are eating!"

Will leaned in toward Mr. Sorjenson. "So, what is the most important thing for Harmony Farms. I mean, what thing do they absolutely need before they can go operational?"

Mr. Sorjeson ran his hand through his white hair and made it stand up funny. "Guess that'd have to be the lagoons. They have to have a large collection pond for all the excrement. It's supposed to be lined a certain way to prevent seepage, but they often skimp on that during construction. But they can't start up without puttin' on a show of tryin' to manage the hundreds of thousands of tons of pig waste."

Will kicked Elizabeth under the table. She knew they must be thinking the same thing! He made wide eyes at her and then winked. Elizabeth hardly heard anything else that was said during the rest of the meal. She was seeing a plan unfold in her mind. Right before Will left, she grabbed his shoulder, pulled him down close and whispered, "I know where I'm gonna hit 'em! But I need your help." He flashed her a quick 'OK' sign with his thumb and forefinger and left.

That night, lying in between the cool cotton sheets, hearing Maizey snore beside her bed, Elizabeth felt the most relaxed she had in weeks. They had a plan! Although she needed Will to execute it, for once she would get to be the muscle.

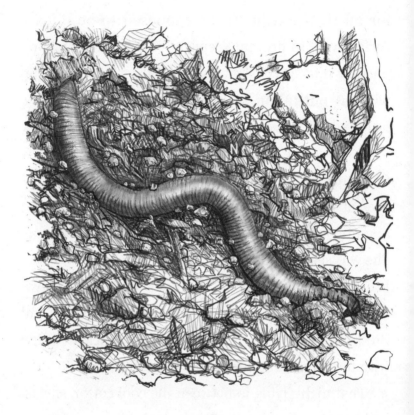

32
Seeing is Believing

The next day Elizabeth had the pleasure of swinging her legs out of bed and rubbing them on Maizey's side. The dog grunted with happiness. By the time they went down to the kitchen, her parents and Mr.

Sorjeson were finishing up their breakfast and heading into the office with a pot of coffee. Her mother stopped long enough to tell her they would be busy most of the day.

"Elizabeth, I don't want you to think we're ignoring you, but tonight's town meeting is very important. Your father and I are going to look at Mr. Sorjeson's presentation and add to it. We've got to do our best job. You are free to fish or pick berries or watch TV, or whatever you want today; just try not to disturb us, OK?"

"No problem!" Elizabeth couldn't believe such a stroke of luck! She would be free to really dig into the dirt and practice. She wanted to be ready and be able to show Will what could be done.

She took Maizey and went to the far end of the garden. There, a large section was lying fallow. Once every five years a quadrant of the garden was left alone and nothing was purposefully grown there. Her father had explained that it allowed the soil to rest up and get balanced. Elizabeth was beginning to under-stand the wisdom of such a practice. Although they were not making money from that area this year, it would grow better vegetables next year and, in a way, make more money.

She sat cross-legged and placed her palms on the ground. She closed her eyes and began to breathe deeply, sending her inquiry into the ground. *Are you there? Who is there?* She began to be aware of the thousands of earthworms wriggling along, opening airways and waterways through the soil. She sensed the tiny creatures that were hard at work digesting the remains of last year's garden. The soil was warm with life. Elizabeth decided to try an experiment.

A few feet away there was a rock about the size of a softball. She reached out her attention and intention. She silently asked the creatures below it to move and allow the rock to come down into their world. The rock began to sink from sight. Elizabeth smiled to herself, but kept her thought bent on the rock. She could sense the dark earth around it. She called it toward her and called it upward.

Little by little, she pulled it toward her and eventually brought it back up into the light of the August day.

Elizabeth spent the next hour moving this rock around the fallow area of the garden, beginning to understand the role that the millions of creatures of the earth played in the texture and stability of the soil.

By the time the sun reached its peak for the day, Elizabeth was exhausted and hungry. She went into the cool of the kitchen, gave Maizey her noontime pills (she washed her hands, because they became covered in dog slobber in the process), and then made herself a big, sweet blackcap fool.

Elizabeth took the blackcaps, which were really black raspberries, from the refrigerator and placed them in a bowl over buttered bread. On top of the bread and blackcaps she sprinkled a teaspoon of sugar and then poured evaporated milk over the whole delicious mess. It was like a taste of heaven. Elizabeth savored the tartness of the berries in contrast with the sweetness of the bread, butter and milk. She felt her strength returning.

She was drinking the last of the purple sweetened milk from the bottom of the bowl when Will came in. He gave a quick glance around and said in a low voice,

"Where can we go to talk?"

Elizabeth took him down to the bridge that crossed Sing Song Creek. She figured they could stand in the middle, over the cool of the water, and see anyone who approached from either side.

Will seemed excited, "Well Lizard Breath, I think I know what you have in mind. Can you show me?"

Elizabeth nodded, but glanced around nervously. *So near the creek? Where is Maizey? What if I make the bridge fall?* All these thoughts passed through her mind while Will looked at her with expectation in his eyes.

"I have to have my hands or my bare feet on the ground. Let's go up to the sheep pasture."

Once again she was high in the pasture, near the woods. She sat cross-legged on the ground with Will and Maizey sitting beside her. "OK. See that big rock?" She pointed to the edge of the ravine where a rock about the size of a basketball was. Will nodded.

Elizabeth set about sending her thoughts and mind down into the earth. She was surprised at how different the population of the hillside soil was than the garden. There were many more rocks and the addition of sheep poop to the pasture made the population of microscopic transformers seem like a whole different culture. It was like going into a city. It took Elizabeth longer than she expected to navigate this new terrain.

She finally felt the underside of the rock and set about pulling it downward and toward them. It took a lot of work. These little critters were more tightly packed than in the garden and there were many more stones to move aside. Finally, the grass in front of them began to push upward, and up rose the rock.

Will was wide-eyed and pale. Although the day was hot, he let out a shiver. "Lizzy, that's incredible! How do you do that?"

She shrugged. "I just ask. I don't know how else to explain it."

Will shook his head once or twice as if to clear his vision. He reached out and placed his hands on the rock. After a moment, he lifted it and carried it back to its place alongside the ravine.

When he came back, he sat and said, "You're amazing. This is going to work! We have to be extra careful, because if anyone from Harmony Farms sees me with you, or around any of the places we are going to hit, they might figure I have something to do with it. Now, let's work out our plan."

33
The Plan

For the next half-hour they worked out the details of what they would do. Any place that Harmony Farms began to excavate for lagoons or shed foundations, Elizabeth was going to go in the night and shake and shift it around. Will had looked at the maps and the plans and knew which nights she had to go where.

"Why at night?" she asked.

"Because no one will be there."

"Oh. How do I get there?" She thought he would say he would drive her.

"I've been thinking about that. A truck driving in or out might be seen. I thought about walking, but that would take a long time and your parents might notice you're gone. Do you think you could do your tree traveling thing?"

Elizabeth hadn't thought of that. So that was a useful skill after all! She thought about how it would be going to a strange place. She wasn't sure how she would ask to be there. An idea came.

"Will, go over the hill to your land and pull a twig off one of the trees, a twig with at least three leaves. Try to pick one that has nice wide branches I can climb down out of. Bring it back. I need to try something."

Will didn't ask a single question. He rose and set off at a jog up the hill and disappeared into the trees. While she waited, Elizabeth stroked Maizey's warm fur and thought about all the work that was ahead of her. She would have to sneak out of the house again. She would be going to strange worksites and working with strange soil. She wrapped her hand around her ankle, and felt she could do it.

When Will came back, he carried a twig from a maple tree. It had three leaves on it and Elizabeth was surprised to see that one of them was beginning to turn red around the edges. She looked at the lengthening shadows of the afternoon, signaling the beginning of the end of the day and realized that this maple leaf was signaling the beginning of the end of the most extraordinary summer. Soon she would have to go back to school.

"Let's hope this works," she said to Will. "Hold onto Maizey."

She strode up to the edge of the woods and the familiar white birch that marked the entrance to the wooded path. She twirled the maple twig in her right hand, smelled it, and closed her eyes. She leaned back against the birch and visualized the three maple leaves in her hand. She focused on the texture and the smell of those leaves. *Please, send me to this beautiful maple tree.* She wanted to laugh out loud as the now familiar tugging and pulling began. This was going to work!

It took her a moment to figure out how to climb down out of the unfamiliar tree. It was a pretty high drop from the lowest branch. Luckily, her dad had taught her long ago that her knees were shock absorbers and she allowed them to bend low as she landed.

She leaned against the trunk of the maple and smiled at the alarm calls the blue jays were sending up. After a few minutes, Maizey came bounding up to her, Will close on her fuzzy heels. He was laughing and Maizey was dancing in happy circles.

"It worked! This will work!" Will might have been eighteen, but he looked as happy as an eight-year-old on Christmas morning.

"Do me a favor though. Try to pick trees that have their lowest branch a little lower than that!" She gestured upward.

"Sorry about that. I wasn't thinking about a shorty like you having to get down!" He stuck out his tongue at her.

She stuck hers out at him and then they hugged and danced and laughed. *Look out Harmony Farms!*

34
G G

The next morning, the mood at the table was mixed. Elizabeth could hardly contain her excitement and enthusiasm for the series of tasks ahead. Her parents, on the other hand, were more glum than she had seen them all summer, even more than after Maizey was lost. (Elizabeth was so happy not to have to say *after Maizey was killed*.)

Mr. Sorjeson, who had stayed in the spare bedroom, came shuffling in. "I would say, 'mornin' folks', 'cept I know it ain't a good mornin'." He poured his coffee and leaned against the kitchen counter.

Elizabeth stopped eating her cereal and looked back and forth from her mother to her father. She had forgotten about the big meeting the night before. She was about to ask how it went when she realized that the very loud silence that was wrapped around the table like a muffler told the whole story.

Mr. Sorjeson began to butter a piece of toast. "I'd like to say I'm surprised. But I ain't. I've seen it too many times. Folks get the glitter of gold in their eyes and they just get blind to reason." He chewed thoughtfully. "Maybe I shoulda worn my really stinky barn coat."

Elizabeth's mother sighed, then looked at Elizabeth and paused. "Elizabeth Angier, what on earth are you grinning about?"

Elizabeth's mind did a rapid search for a response that wouldn't cause more questions. "Uh, I'm excited that school is going to start up soon."

Mr. Sorjeson laughed. "You must be one of those smart kids. I ain't never heard of a lil'un that was excited about going back to school!" He stood up and brushed his hands on his pants. To save her or either of her parents from having to say anything, she jumped up. "I gotta go help Will with something."

Mr. Sorjeson reached out and shook her hand. "I got's ta' get goin' as well. It's been a pleasure meeting you folks. Wish I coulda been more persuasive. You've got all my contacts now. Keep up the good fight!"

Elizabeth thought that for a stinky guy, he was really nice. *Don't worry Mr. Stinky, I am definitely going to give 'em a good fight!*

Before Elizabeth bolted out the door, she noticed that for the first time in her young life, her father was rude. He didn't thank Mr. Sorjeson or get up to see him out. He just sat and stared at his bowl of uneaten and now soggy cereal. He hadn't even touched his coffee.

As planned, Will was already up in the platform in

The Scout. He had several pieces of paper. Each had a map photocopied on it and also had a twig with three or four leaves taped to it. Elizabeth didn't know what the maps were of, but she did a quick inventory: birch, maple, oak, oak, pine; she stopped.

"A pine tree! Will! That's gonna hurt!"

He shrugged. "There wasn't anything else there, Lizzy. I swear!"

She sighed and made a mental note to wear long pants and a long sleeved shirt when she did that one. "What are these dates?"

"I put the dates I thought would be best for you to go. Assume you are going after midnight. So the date you see is sorta for the next day, in a way."

"After midnight? How do you think I'm going to manage to stay awake that long?"

He gave her a long hard stare. "Because you will. I know you. I know there's nothing more important to you than making sure that at this time next year you are still sitting out at the picnic table under The Chaplain, eating ear after ear of corn on the cob. I know you want to keep picking mushrooms and keep swimming in the creek. You will do it because you have to."

The way he said it, so cold and matter of fact, it sounded as hard and steely as the knife tied to her ankle. Will was right, of course. She couldn't imagine life at Three Oaks with the stinging acrid smell and the flies and the screams of tortured pigs. She could barely allow herself to imagine what would happen if the Town of Avon succeeded in taking their farm to build the new Harmony Farms offices. The only thing she was going to allow herself to imagine from this point forward was one successful Gaia Girl mission after another.

"Will, this one," she held up one of the papers with an oak twig taped to it. "This one is dated for tomorrow."

"No, Lizard Breath. After midnight, tomorrow becomes today. They've leveled out the foundations over at the Danners'. It's already started. Are you ready?"

She turned and sent her gaze out over the valley below. She could see the tops of The Sentry and The

Chaplain, waving in the breeze. She could hear the low call of the sheep in the pasture. She could smell the unique smell of the field of pumpkins wafting up from below. She could also hear the growl and burping of the diesel engines from the west.

She bent down and drew her knife from its now familiar place at her ankle. She knelt, and using the tip of her knife she carved G G into the wood of the platform. She brushed her hand over the letters a couple of times. She liked the way the letters felt new in the old wood. She sheathed her knife and stood.

"I'm ready."

35
Mission: Danner Farm

Elizabeth sat in the dark of her room, listening to Maizey's snoring and fighting against sleep. She had placed a rubber band around her wrist and every time her eyelids felt heavy, she gave it a snap and snapped herself back to wakefulness. She looked at the map Will had given her. SNAP! She thought about the oak tree at the corner of what used to be the Danner's house. SNAP! She hoped that she would be able to climb down.

When, finally, her parents came upstairs to their bedroom, she had to wait almost an hour more until their voices stopped coming low through the wall. SNAP! She had to wait even longer after that to make sure they had gone to sleep. SNAP! She then took the rubber band off. She was now very nervous and wide awake.

For the second time that summer, she took the screen out of her window. Maizey picked up her head for a moment, but after Elizabeth assured her, she flopped her big shaggy head back onto the floor with a thud. Again, Elizabeth made her way, barefooted, down the length of the porch roof and into the boughs of The Chaplain. She climbed down to the familiar trunk and leaned back. From her pocket she pulled the oak twig from the Danner farm. She stared at the pattern of the veins in the leaves. She smelled its unique smell. She leaned back and asked The Chaplain to send her there. Moments later, she was navigating the Danners' oak to the ground.

She dropped to the ground and caught her breath. Ahead of her in the gloom of the late summer night were the looming shapes of monsters. *Not monsters, you silly Lizzy: construction equipment!* In the dark, the backhoes and earthmovers looked large and menacing. Elizabeth took her knife out, gripped the handle tightly, and began to move her bare feet.

She moved around the dark equipment, half expecting one of them to leap to life with a growl. She still had a vivid picture of such machines clawing down the buildings in this very spot. She saw the first foundation.

There was an area almost as large as her big barn dug down about four feet. Already there were several pipes leading out from the large rectangle. Elizabeth decided to investigate and discovered that they had begun to shape what must be one of the lagoons. *I can't believe how close it is to Sing Song Creek! Don't they know it floods up this high sometimes?*

Elizabeth stopped herself from wasting time thinking mean thoughts about Harmony Farms. She went back up to the first foundation and sat down in the dirt. She placed her hands on the cool soil and began to focus. It made her sad. This dirt was almost dead. There were less than a quarter of the creatures she normally felt. They were slow and hungry and could not hear her. She began to feel a little nervous. Would her efforts get out of control again?

C'mon! You're a Gaia Girl! she thought. She stopped to lift her knife up high in her right hand and drive it into the dirt up to the handle. Now she felt committed.

She began to sift and sort and move the soil. The smooth walls of the foundation began to patter down and the rectangle began to lose its defined shape. She finally decided to give the westward wall a big tug. It fell inward with a rush. There was a horrible moment when she thought things were starting to go out of control again.

The crumbling continued to move westward and by the time Elizabeth knew what was happening a backhoe was beginning to lean over on its side, like a ship that was taking on water. Elizabeth quickly marshaled what little strength was in the soil and pushed it back upright.

Now she felt strong! She had just moved one of the big, belching monsters! She had an idea and a little, wicked grin crept across her face. She let the backhoe tip back onto its side. *It's not broken, but they sure will be quick to notice something happened!*

She spent another hour going to the other six shed foundations and either sunk them ridiculously deep or practically filled them in! She stirred up a few tunneling moles and she swore they gave her dirty looks as they scampered off into the night. She ended at the lagoon.

She stood for a while and listened to the night song. The creek was still singing its unending happy tune. Although the creek had almost taken lives this summer, Elizabeth knew that it wasn't a force to be feared; it was a marvel to be protected. She ended up clearing back the bank of the creek until the Sing Song waters swirled into the lagoon area. The water filled it like a swimming pool. She created an outflow that allowed the water to run back downhill into the familiar banks.

Elizabeth became aware that birds were stirring in the branches of the trees around her. Far off, she heard the mourning doves begin their pre-dawn serenade. She was exhausted, but realized there was one more thing that needed to be done.

Where the Danners' driveway met the road, there was a big wooden sign with the Harmony Farms logo on it. COMING SOON! It blared. There was a phone number for anyone interested in working for them. Elizabeth stared hard at the logo, thinking about how thousands of happy red barns, green pastures, and families, like hers, that lived on such farms were being replaced by the smell and the pain and poison of CAFOs.

From her heart, to her feet and into the soil ran her disgust. The sign began to sink into the ground. Soon, it disappeared altogether. But it wasn't enough to swallow up that lie. Elizabeth strained to tell the transformers in the soil what she wanted to do. Her mind ached with it.

After a time, the two legs of the sign reappeared. Elizabeth smiled. She knew that down below, the bright sun that arched over the barn had been blackened and that the ONY of the word Harmony had been stripped away. It now read, COMING SOON! HARM   FARMS. The sign now told the truth. And, if anyone looked closely, which she was sure they wouldn't, at the end of each leg of the sign there was etched a small G.

Mission Accomplished.

36
Too Costly

In the remaining weeks before school began, Elizabeth and Will worked together to make Harmony Farms' plans fail to move forward. Elizabeth was bone tired. It took almost a week and a half to cover the five major sites.

At the Smith farm, she discovered the Smith family dog! It had taken all her energy to do what she had to do while simultaneously asking the trees around the farm to drop branches and make noises to distract the dog. He ended up dashing off into the woods while she dashed about, filling in the dreaded lagoons and dismantling the foundations.

As anticipated, the pine tree proved painful, but she learned a fantastic fact while there. She had just climbed down and was under the canopy of pine boughs when a truck pulled in! A man went into the trailer and a light went on. Elizabeth held the trunk of the pine and thought: *Does anyone ever come under here?*

To her complete amazement, an answer came to her. She was still holding the pine's trunk and into her mind came a parade of pictures of just who had come into the cover of the pine: a deer seeking shelter from the rain, a stray cat that had nestled into the fallen needles and slept, a group of turkeys, two giggling children, a kissing couple. Although she knew she could travel through trees, Gaia had failed to inform her she could see and hear their stories as well. This was really Tree T.V.! She had wanted to keep watching, but the man had left and she had to be satisfied with the view of the Harmony Farms mobile office trailer rolling over on its side.

The headlines of the newspaper blared allegations of "industrial sabotage." However, police could find no evidence of anyone entering the sites. Elizabeth had, after the first night at the Danners', always paused to ask the earth to smooth away her footprints. She did, however, leave a little G G somewhere at each location.

Elizabeth often didn't slip back in through her window until 4 a.m. and it wasn't uncommon for her mother to shake her awake at 5:30 in the morning. She overheard her mother telling her father that Elizabeth must be going through a growth spurt the way she was sleeping! And in a way, Elizabeth was growing. She became more confident in her relationship with the earth beneath her feet. She found some rest and nourishment from immersing herself into Gaia's ever-changing beautiful, green song while she worked those last long hot days of August.

One hot afternoon Elizabeth sat sipping lemonade in the cool shade of The Chaplain. She thought about how many people in her family had done this before her. Then she remembered the pine tree. What kind of stories would The Chaplain have to tell? She leaned her back against the trunk, closed her eyes, and asked.

She saw an older woman in a plain dress come out the back door of her house. She had a school bell in her hand. It was the same school bell her mother used! The woman rang it twice and cupped her hand to her mouth and called "Daaanniel."

A lanky boy came running up from the barn. He was smiling and Elizabeth could tell who it was from the dimples. It was her father!

"Daniel, I want you to go out and pick me some bell peppers before it rains."

"It's not going to rain, Grandma."

"It sure is! I asked The Chaplain this morning and that is what it said."

"I think you're teasing me. What else did The Chaplain tell you?"

The woman seemed to look right at Elizabeth! She smiled a little secret smile and motioned for young Daniel Angier to come sit beside her on the porch step.

"The Chaplain told me it was time to give you this."

From her pocket, she pulled a knife, the old Indian knife!

"Wow!" young Daniel cried. He turned it over and over in his hands.

"Your great grandfather made that. It is important to know where you come from Daniel. Someone from our family has always lived here and I hope that some-one always will."

"I'm not going anywhere, Grandma."

"I hope not! This soil is in your blood. You belong here. Take good care of that. You may want to pass it on to your own children. Now, go get me those peppers."

The boy ran off and the woman rose from the step. She looked over her shoulder toward Elizabeth with a jokester's grin on her face.

And then the memory was over. Elizabeth was standing, looking at her back door. She turned and hugged The Chaplain. "Thank you." A low chuckle came tumbling down through the branches.

It was peak season for Three Oaks and her days were filled with picking, washing, and boxing produce. Will was often there, working beside her. As they loaded boxes into the truck one blistering hot afternoon, Elizabeth noticed that her father was laughing and joking with her and Will. When had he started laughing and joking again? Had she been too tired to notice the change?

When the last box was loaded in, he paused to drink from the pump by the garden shed. He wiped the back of his hand across his mouth. "Ahhh! Elizabeth, this is the best water in New York State!"

"And it's going to stay that way, right Mr. Angier?" Will said, his voice bright and happy.

Elizabeth looked back and forth between the two tall men.

"Did you tell her?" Her father asked the question to Will, right over the top of her head.

"Tell me what? Tell me what?"

"You tell her, sir. You're the one that has worked so

hard fighting this."

Her father sat on the running board of the truck and grinned fit to split.

"Rumor has it that Harmony Farms is pulling out! Their accountants say stabilizing the land is going to be too costly and too time consuming."

"Pulling out? Like, leaving for good?" To Elizabeth, everything--her breathing, her heartbeat and even Gaia's green song--seemed to stop as she waited for his reply.

"That's right kiddo!" He jumped up, grabbed her under the armpits, and swung her up and around. She shrieked. He hadn't done such a thing since she was little and much lighter.

Will scratched his head and put a comical, confused look on his face. "I can't figure why those folks had so much trouble digging around here."

Elizabeth looked at him out of the corners of her eyes and tried not to laugh.

Her father said, "That is a mystery. I hear the town council has asked the USGS to come up and do a complete survey to make sure the whole town isn't going to sink into the earth or something."

"You know what I think?" Elizabeth ventured.

"What's that, kiddo?"

"I think that your Grandma Elizabeth got mad. You said our blood was in the soil. I bet she wouldn't have wanted a big stinkin' pig farm next door!"

Her father laughed and hugged her. He held her out at arm's length. His eyes were crinkled and his dimples were deep. "That's the smartest answer I have heard anyone give yet!"

Maizey gave a big "WOOF" in agreement.

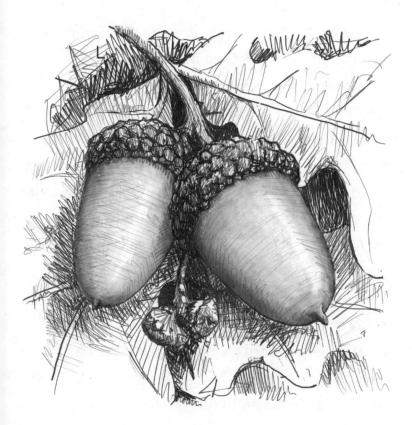

37
Endings & Beginnings

Two days before school started back up, it was official. Harmony Farms was leaving. They were going to auction off the land they had bought. When Elizabeth saw the headlines on the kitchen counter, she almost started crying. But instead, she gave herself an inward grin that, if she had looked in the mirror, dimpled her cheeks much like her father's! She smiled inward and could hear Will's voice, *"You go, Gaia Girl!"*

It had been the worst summer of her life, but in a lot of ways, it had also been the best. As she sliced up that morning's bread, she noticed how much taller and stronger she felt. When she heard her mother on the telephone asking Will to come over the hill to help that day, she didn't feel mad at all. Will was a true friend. Will was no longer a 'rent-a-brother', but a real brother-in-arms.

After all, it wasn't a 'rent-a-son' that had saved their farm. It had been her. Well, her and Gaia; actually, her and Gaia and Will. She thought that maybe any successful superhero mission was much like Gaia herself; dependent on cooperation and balance; many parts, many roles, all working together to accomplish something.

She came home from her first day of fifth-grade happy and excited. Mr. Toski was super duper nice and he said they were going to be learning some earth science that year. She hoped that what she learned would help her understand Gaia better.

She came in the front door and almost ran into Will, who was coming out of her parents' office. She was surprised; she had never seen Will anywhere but out on the farm and in the kitchen. Her parents came out behind him. They all had big secret smiles on their faces.

"What?" Elizabeth demanded. She punched Will's arm. "C'mon Buffalo Breath! What's the big story here?"

Her father slung his arm around Will's shoulder. "Meet the Chief Operations Officer of the newly formed subsidiary of Three Oaks Farm."

"Huh?" Elizabeth was confused. "What is a subsidiary?"

"Just like an oak drops an acorn to make a new tree, a company can drop a baby company to try to grow and expand. Will is going to run Acorn Acres."

"Acorn Acres!" Her mother boomed out, sounding like a television commercial. "Healthy and humane eggs and poultry. Free range, no hormones, and delivered directly to the finest New York City restaurants!"

"Lizzy!" Will said. "My parents had a bit of money and your parents had the rest to buy the Danner place at the Harmony Farms' auction! I'm going to be part owner and the, what was it again?" Will turned toward her parents.

"Chief Operations Officer," her mother said.

Will wrinkled his nose. "Sounds too corporate for my taste. How 'bout just, Happy Chicken Man?"

Elizabeth laughed. "Oh yeah! I can definitely call you that!"

Her father ushered them all into the kitchen. "I was thinking we had to celebrate in a unique Three Oaks/Acorn Acres kind of way." He stroked his chin. "What do you say I take my new partner and my best gardener, via inner tube, downstream, then downriver to Gino's Diner in Avon?"

Elizabeth cheered, Will cheered, and Maizey let out a "WOOF".

"Oh no, Maizey." Her mother said. "No more creek rides for you! You're staying here with me. You can go for a ride in the truck when they call for their ride back!"

It was the best afternoon Elizabeth ever had. They joked and splashed and talked about the plans for the new farm. Elizabeth couldn't believe that Will would be living and working right next door! She lay back in her tube and enjoyed the happy, wild music all around her, which today, finally, included the laughter of Will and her father.

Because the water was much lower that time of year, the delta where Sing Song Creek dumped into the Avon River was a wide expanse of squishy mud with gurgling channels through it. As they squished along, laughing at the sucking and farting noises the mud made, her father suddenly said, "Hold still!"

They all froze and looked where he was looking. "See! There in the shade of those poplars. An otter! I don't think I've seen an otter since I was about eight!" His face was open and wide with happiness and wonder.

To the amazement of all, except maybe Elizabeth, the otter rose and waved one wee paw at them.

Tucked into the green song in Elizabeth's ears came

a high, sparkling voice that sounded like all the stars in the sky laughing with contentment. "You did it, dear heart! I can already feel a sense of ease returning to the trees. Rest up, there are more dire things happening. I have more powers to give you, and you have much more to learn. Soon you will meet the others, and it will be time to help save me."

THE END. . .

. . . AND

THE BEGINNING OF GAIA GIRLS

www.gaiagirls.com

Afterword

A few thoughts on what is real and what isn't.

There is a real place called Avon, NY. That is not the place I wrote about. The real Avon is on the western side of New York State and it is fairly flat. I have never actually pulled off I-390 in Avon; I simply liked the sound of the name. The place I wrote about would have to be further to the east, possibly in the Finger Lakes region. The succession of hills and valleys is beautiful and interesting and it was what my mind's eye was looking at while I wrote.

There is a real group called Harmony Valley Farms. I didn't know this until after I wrote the book. I am pleased to say that Harmony Valley Farms is a group of organic farmers in the midwest. I met some of them in Chicago, and they love Gaia and treat her well.

The name Elizabeth was inspired by my Aunt Elizabeth. She grew up on the same farm I did and now resides in Michigan. She brightened my childhood with all her knowledge of the flora and fauna on our farm.

The name Will was inspired by her son, my cousin. Will was the fearless snake-catcher and expert salamander-racer. We spent many happy hours ramming around the farm together. The highlight of my summer was when the cousins came from Michigan.

Are factory farms real? You bet your bacon they are! I

read a book called "The Meat You Eat" by Ken Midkiff. The images haunted me. I changed my meat-buying habits immediately. You can see pictures of real factory farms (and that includes chicken, beef and dairy too) at www.gracelinks.org.

As someone who cares about the earth, I get upset when I read about people or corporations that break down the systems we rely on for food, water and air. However, I would never destroy personal property. Thinking up Gaia powers for Elizabeth was fun, but in reality we must employ different powers. Gaia power can be wielded with the wallet. How we spend our money, essentially what we say 'yes' to, and who we elect as stewards of public commons, will have the biggest impact on Gaia's health.

I hope you visit the Gaia Girls website: www.gaiagirls.com You will learn more about Gaia and what you can do to help her. We have made a lot of fun games and puzzles. You can read some "deleted scenes" and maybe even get a sneak preview of the second Gaia Girls book, "Way of Water!"

Does Gaia really talk? I think she does, if you are willing to listen. You also have to be willing to pick up her language: a scolding blue jay, a gust of wind, the rattle of leafless branches can all tell you something about what is going on around you.

Just listen.

Eco Audit

Daisyworld Press and Gaia Girls have worked very hard to pick products that make sense. We've voted with our dollars to save trees and natural resources as we publish the Gaia Girls Book Series.

NEW LEAF PAPER
ENVIRONMENTAL BENEFITS STATEMENT

Gaia Girls: Enter the Earth is printed on New Leaf EcoBook 100, made with 100% post-consumer waste, processed chlorine free. By using this environmental paper, Daisyworld Press saved the following resources:

trees	water	energy	solid waste	greenhouse gases
70 fully grown	30,156 gallons	34 million BTUs	1,963 pounds	4,006 pounds

Calculated based on research done by Environmental Defense and other members of the Paper Task Force.

© New Leaf Paper   www.newleafpaper.com   888.989.5323

Here are some other things that benefit from using 100% post-consumer recycled paper. In one year the seventy trees we saved in this first printing will produce 18,200 pounds of oxygen. That means 140 people are supported by the oxygen that our saved trees will produce. Each year our saved trees will absorb about 700 pounds of air pollutants, including 280 pounds of ozone and 210 pounds of particulates. Wow! It just proves that we really do vote with our dollars. So remember, think before you shop: Gaia will appreciate it!

Hidden Pictures & Codes

Elizabeth discovered there is a whole hidden world in Gaia's soil. That is why we have hidden things for you to find!

If you look carefully at the cover illustration, you will find hidden items buried in the soil. How many did you find? Come to www.gaiagirls.com to see if you're right!

Within the beautiful illustrations of flora and fauna from Upstate New York, there are hidden codes! However, there are codes in only thirty-six of the thirty-seven chapter illustrations. What chapter doesn't have a code?

See if you can solve this puzzle by finding the hidden letters in each chapter illustration. The number under the space is the chapter you should look at.

___ ___ ___ ___ ___ before you ___ ___ ___ ___
12   1   22 32 13   3   1   25 5

and help ___ ___ ___ ___ ___ ___ ___ Gaia.
          5   28 25 12 6   18 12

At www.gaiagirls.com you can solve other puzzles and games that require using your copy of "Enter the Earth" and your best puzzle solving skills. You can also play Gaia Girls arcade games. Daisyworld Press believes that Gaia Girls-Enter the Earth is Fiction with a Mission!

Go to www.gaiagirls.com to learn more about your mission!

Coming Next!

Gaia ❧ Girls
Way of Water

www.gaiagirls.com